ISBN: 979-8-866-79634-2

To my ever-supportive family

Chapter One

S he looked so peaceful when she slept. So free of worry and clear of any shackles of reality. The way she smiled, I suspected a beautiful dream had befallen her, at-long-last! But just as I hoped that nothing would wake her up so soon, the doorbell rang. She slumped out of bed and with a deep sigh she made her way to the door.

I knew what was about to come, so I followed her and rested my hand on her shoulder. She swung the door open. A young man in a suit that was clearly too large for him, greeted her, "Good morning, Miss Lisa Francys. Mr. Bernet could not make it today, so I am here on his behalf."

"Are you here regarding my appeal?" Lisa answered covering her eyes from the blinding morning sun.

"Yes, could I come in and discuss it with you?"

"I do not have the strength to go through all this again. Just tell me the verdict."

"I must advise you to be patient and -"

"Can I get my kids back or not?" she snapped.

"I am sorry to inform you that - " That was all she had to hear before slamming the door. The young man knocked the door repeatedly, hoping she would reconsider, but to Lisa his knocking was just background noise.

Lisa sat at the kitchen table, staring at the cracks on the wall. I joined her. I was surprised, she did not feel any pain. I could only describe it as emptiness – she felt no emotion at all. Her blank stare and hunched body were one with a hopeless soul. Just then I wished I could hug her tightly, letting her know that there was someone who loved her deeply.

"Why me?" she whispered. "I just want Martha and George back, is that too much to ask?"

From everything I have witnessed, seeing her throw objects and furniture around in utter despair, destroying the kitchen, was where even I felt hopeless.

She laid on the cold tiles, among broken plates and glass, for hours. This was the moment where I knew that this was just the beginning.

The rest of the week was a cycle of misery, repetitive and bland. Heck, she didn't even leave the house. I was with her every second, stranded in this place I have never been before. I felt I was fading away, like a statue slowly erased by droplets of rain. My sickness was getting worse, and I couldn't do anything else except love her as much as I always did.

I stood uselessly in the hallway and watched the neighbours walk by. A newly married couple with a four-year-old. I smiled gratefully at them, but of course they did not see me.

Lisa brusquely rushed past me and unlocked the door, walking out of the house with intent and purpose. Naturally I followed her. It was a sunny afternoon, where the smell of fresh grass invaded your nostrils and where seagulls floated in the breeze. It was the same gentle breeze that greeted us on our little endeavour. Yet in the middle of all this beauty, we dragged with us our sorrow. We stood out like a grey hair.

Lisa made her way to the closest corner shop. "Two bottles of wine and some of those ramen packets, please."

"White or red?" the elderly store clerk asked, vigorously waving a plastic bag to open it.

"Red. Oh, and give me some of these doughnuts over there," tapping the glass vitrine.

"That will be twenty-four pounds and ninety-nine pence."

Lisa paid by pushing the paper bills heavily into the open palm of the clerk. After stuffing the change deep in her pockets, she made her way out. I wasn't particularly happy of how she behaved, but at least she was out of the house. It might do her good.

She opened one of the wine bottles and started to sip it. At a park nearby she sat down on a bench.

The park was exceptionally silent, without a person in sight. I couldn't sense any threat nearby, so I sat down next to her instead of patrolling her surroundings as I usually did.

I held on to her hand which she leaned on her lap. A butterfly, from one of the nearby bushes, flew in and landed on her hand as well. To my surprise she started talking. She usually talks to herself a lot, but this time it seemed she was talking to me.

"I need you right now. Whatever you are, I need your help."

Lisa was an atheist, she always frowned upon the idea of something outside earthly reality. It didn't change the love I had for her one bit, but it was nice to hear something like that without a sarcastic remark or for the opening line of a joke.

"I can't handle it anymore. I don't know what to do," she said sipping her wine and scratching off the paper label on it.

Suddenly I felt weird. My skin prickled and with every breath I felt something deep inside me flourish. Like a sprouting seed in dying soil. As I looked up, I noticed a squirrel on a tree trunk, completely motionless - so are the leaves mid-air and the birds' song was cut short too. Time stopped. The silence was deafening.

With her eyes closed she began saying in a quiet and hesitant tone, "Is anyone there? I'm sorry, but I don't know any prayers. I hope you haven't left me yet. I know I am not the most loving, most just, or perfect. But do I really deserve all of this? If you are so powerful you know my situation, then why don't you help me? At least this once?"

"But I was always here," I blurted out.

Lisa raised her head as if she had heard me. After a longer moment of silence, she opened her eyes and said in the sincerest tone I have ever heard from her, "Thank you". The squirrel darted into the bushes, and the bird began chirping again. I stopped glowing.

She then stood up and with all the things she bought, she went home. Another wasted evening.

While she slept on the couch with the second bottle in her hand, I stood guard.

I felt something sinister approaching.

The apartment above had been abandoned since Lisa moved in, but the ceiling began to creak. The curtains in the living room began to flail, but the air remained still. I got up from the couch and stood in front of Lisa. I summoned my spear and shield. Out the hallway came a *Buralag*. A demon who thrived in those tempted by evil. It had come to feast.

It had grown considerable since the last time we met. Its claws had become thick and sharp. No longer was it lanky. The eyes gave out a more pungent hatred.

"Begone, or shall I remind you who you came to rival," I said, pointing at it with my spear.

"She sleeps so soundly, like a small baby," the Buralag growled. "She doesn't look as strong as she used to be. Neither do you."

"Still strong enough to defeat you," I said, hoping it would not call my bluff.

The lock of the front door turned. Lisa's mother, an elderly woman with a love of sporadically visiting her daughter, came in. She immediately dropped her purse and rushed to Lisa when she saw the surrounding mess.

"Not again my dear," she said helping Lisa up. She threw the wine bottle across the living room and got some water. Lisa, who could barely collect her thoughts, drank the water.

The Buralag shrieked in pain, beginning to faint in power.

"Look at you. So mad with evil, but you get beaten by a simple glass of water," I smirked.

It didn't like my comment and went straight for me. I took a quick step to the side in an attempt to juke its charge. It hurled past me, but its claws took a hold of the side of my shield pulling me with it with immense force. I flapped my wings to regain my balance and with my spear I pierced its back. It shrieked again. I was relieved, but I couldn't pull out my spear. The Buralag pulled my spear deeper into its body, like quicksand. I let go and took a step back while the Buralag rose up. Without hesitation it swung its long, left arm at me. I blocked its blow with my shield, but its right arm took the chance and flung across my face, engraving its disgusting claws along my cheek. I fell down.

The Buralag looked over me and said, "Not that dangerous without your spear are you now. You pitifull bastard."

I could feel blood pouring from my cheek into my mouth.

The Buralag reached into his chest cavity and pulled out my spear. It then jumped on me with a short run up. But I flung myself up, feet first, kicking him down. Now the Buralag was on the floor, my spear flew from its claws out of reach for both of us. I flew up quickly and hurled down in a short free fall, beheading it with my shield.

The fight was over. The Buralag lay there, burning into oblivion.

I couldn't do this for much longer. I never saw it so ferocious. They all are evolving, but me. I reckoned as long as I tried my best, it would be enough, because there was nothing I wouldn't do for Lisa. She just laid there, while her mother cleaned up her mess.

After a couple hours, Lisa came to herself. She saw her mother whizzing about the kitchen.

"What are you doing?" Lisa asked her, trying to sharpen her blurry vision.

"I am cleaning the kitchen. I don't want you to impale yourself on one of those massive plate chunks," her mum said.

"It is fine as it is. You don't have to help, I know that you have your session today."

"No, it is alright. It isn't for another hour. Something told me to come give you a visit and I am so happy I did," her mother said while sweeping the remainder of broken cups and ripped cookbooks into a neat pile.

Lisa sat up from her red couch, giving out a deep grunt. I could not make out how she felt. It was a mixture of disappointment and gratefulness, I thought. She broke out in tears.

"Mum, please forgive me. I-I can't handle it anymore. Day by day I can feel myself go off the rails more and more. My therapist is a dickhead and everything I truly love is in Tony's hands. I am a failure."

Her mother stopped cleaning. The broom was leaned on the kitchen island, while she walked toward her daughter.

"You know you are always welcome to join my class. I do realise we've had this conversation many times, about faith that is. But I would love for you to come and join."

Lisa's eyes looked up to her mother, who stood right before her.

"I'm not sure," Lisa said.

"Just this once," her mother said. "Please."

Lisa really didn't want to go. Despite that she found the energy to stand up and embrace her. "I'll try."

Lisa put her hair in a bun and put on her favourite shirt and jeans. She took Aspirin, as her headache which was annoying her, became more painful. They walked to a building twenty minutes away. It looked more like a garage than a normal house. Its white walls were poorly painted, revealing the naked concrete beneath it in several places. A small window placed infuriatingly off centre was the only opening at the front. The 'front' door was at the back, rather mysteriously.

Her mother opened the door to reveal a humble and warm room with a large wooden table in the middle.

"Sorry for the mess, it gets quite dusty in here. I need to start to find a solution for that," her mother said while brushing her hand along the table. "Would you be a lamb and throw me the cloth behind you?"

"Quite creepy this place I must say," Lisa said throwing her jacket over the chair rest and passing the cloth.

"It's better than nothing," her mother scoffed.

Having straightened up the room, they put candles on the table. They were a set of different colours, apparently donated by some members of the community. Then from a little storage room in the corner, they set up wooden chairs that looked ancient, but the cushion on them was still rot-free and well maintained.

Lisa barely sat down when we all heard the shrill sound of a breaking car.

"I will get them!" her mother exclaimed in excitement, rushing in little cute steps. It was wholesome to see an older person still be excited by something, burning with a passion or interest. Something that Lisa didn't have.

I could tell Lisa was second guessing her decision to come. Whenever she feels stressed, she does this thing where she pinches her arm hair and twists it back and forth. It's rather adorable.

"I am glad you could make it," the door creeks open again. "We have a special guest today, my daughter Lisa," her mother said gesturing towards her. Out came a man with visible tattoos around his neck and the back of his hands. No judgement at all, other than seeming like an intimidating guy. His girlfriend came in after him, in a rather elegant manner. It filled my heart seeing him take care of her, pulling out a seat and holding hands. I could see he was truly happy.

After that, the room started to fill up and the session started once all participants sat down. There were around fifteen of them.

"Good day to you all," Lisa's mother started, clasping her hands together rather tightly. "I hope you had a great weekend, and you are ready for another tutorial. To start off I would like to say that I think of you as brothers and sisters, whose path to God we share. We are all so close, lik- like a family. Well, today I have the special occasion to introduce you all to my lovely daughter Lisa."

Her mind was in such chaos, but I leaned on the wall laughing in hysteria. Her mother presented her like a new product in some type of opening event. Lisa wanted to say many things, but what came out was a *"Hi y'all"*. That voice crack was utter comedy. Of course, I felt bad for laughing, especially how embarrassed she felt afterward, but she was able to laugh it off later on.

Now that Lisa found her 'brothers and sisters', I sat down with them, ready to see what they had to offer.

Everyone was sitting motionless, but eager and attentive. I was impressed. Not often did you see people meet up at a gathering of any kind and be so interested that each of them would have a smile imprinted for the entire thing. I too found myself grinning in anticipation.

Lisa's mother started the tutorial with prayers and good wishes for health and prosperity, especially for one son of the participants who had experienced a stroke and lay in the hospital. She devoted quite some attention towards that. Then she asked all of us to look around the room and appreciate with whom we can share today's tutorial with.

I did take a good look around, but I, for a long time, stared at my lovely Lisa. She was listening with intent, closely, to what her mother was preaching. But I didn't listen to her mother anymore. I kept looking at her. At this very moment I had a need to ask her, but would she answer me even if she could hear me? I guess she would not.

It reminded me of a time, during Lisa's childhood, when she had an imaginary friend. She used to call him Paul. Lisa talked to him whenever she was alone, and she treated him lovingly and fairly. Never did she curse at him, even if she was frustrated at him for not speaking. There were tea parties and duets. Oh, the duets! She established a plan for a song and distributed verses evenly to sing. She had a part and Paul had a part. And by the end she always complemented Paul. Such a sweet child. But in times of difficulty, she used to dream of him hugging her. She didn't have any siblings, nor did she have a lot of friends back then, so the dream of Paul hugging her was just that - a dream. But little did she know that I always hugged her. Little did she know that I always sung the verses that she gave to me. I was the one drinking her marvellous tea, because I was Paul.

Children, especially at such a young age, are so pure that their lack of sins and temptation makes it possible for them to sense me, but once they grow up they stray away. From that moment on, they wouldn't be able to perceive me for the rest of their lives.

These were my favourite experiences. She could actually 'see' me. But this was long in the past. I wished to sing with her one more time, for old times' sake. Come to think of it, she didn't sing at all since she started living by herself. I wondered if her voice changed. Suddenly, Lisa's mother robbed me of that trail of thought.

"May the Lord all mighty bring peace and purify our hearts anew from stains of sins."

All of them were sitting holding hands. It was rather heart-warming to see. Their eyes were pinched close, except for Lisa's. She was looking all around the room, still sceptical of all of this.

But so was I. Normally I could feel it when Lisa resided in places of religious significance. Whenever Lisa went to church during a school trip, I could smell something that was close to me - nostalgic. There the air was light and had a slight taste of wood – dry and earthy. But I didn't feel the same here. Even during their prayer, when I expected a similar experience to the one in the park, nothing happened.

Under the table, her foot was tapping quickly.

"Today's topic at hand that I want to cover is the power of questions," Lisa's mother said. "When was the last time you asked God for something? You might think you do every day, but what I realised is that we don't. Not really. What happens is, we ask God for something, and then do it ourselves. What does that mean?"

Nobody said anything.

"It means we ask about things that we could do ourselves. We love the control of seeing our ask being answered. This is not faith. What I decided to do, is to ask for things *beyond* my reach. Things that seem impossible. So far away, so unreasonable. But this is not all. You have to trust in God *fully*. God will see how much you truly trust Him, when your impossible question is all that you have left. When you lean on Him without any plan B. You have to fully let yourself go."

She pointed at all of us.

"Imagine, right now, your impossible question, your last hope, could be answered. What is that question? I want us to go around the table. Mark, could you go first?"

Everybody scrambled their minds to figure out what to say.

It took Mark a couple moments to do the same. "What I would ask is whether He could cure my father's cancer. It's stage three. Last time we went to the hospital, the doctor looked right at me and said that they couldn't help him anymore. Every day I feel my dad fading from my grasp, and there is nothing I can do about. As you said, it's an impossible ask. God, what are *you* going to do?"

His face turned to one of brokenness. A fear of something that is imminent. Lisa couldn't even glance at him, or at anybody.

"Thank you Mark for sharing. I pray and trust for God's help in your query," Lisa's mother said. "What about you Belle?"

"My kids. I would ask God to show me how to be the best mum I could be - ."

"I'm sorry," Lisa stood up. "I have to leave."

Lisa made her way to the door. Everyone was shocked and only her mother tried to go after her, but she didn't succeed. Lisa left her jacket behind, but she headed home anyway. I could sense she wanted alcohol. That was how Lisa coped with stress and her overall unhappiness, usually. But I couldn't let her drink again, so this time I interrupted.

I am able to 'implant' certain thoughts. They come as just thoughts but are powerful enough to persuade the person otherwise. It usually works, because they think they thought of it themselves. Lisa didn't like to go against her own intuitions.

However, whenever I did this, my power waned and I lost more of my feathers.

"George", I whispered. "George and Marta."

I could see clearly that she then thought of her kids. The only thought stronger than any other. A feather did fall off and transcended to her reality in form of an itch on her head, which she furiously scratched at.

Lisa turned around, speed walking to her ex's house. The sun hid behind a vast group of clouds, bringing a cold shadow onto the streets of the small town. Cars whistled by, workers rushing home to their warm lunch.

As soon as the house was in sight I rushed ahead and peaked inside. I saw no one in the living room, so I flew through the walls to the bedroom. No one. I rushed around covering all two floors and basement, but it was empty. While I was in the basement, through the darkness I saw the cold walls reveal an entrance, that seemed not to belong there. "What is *that?*" I thought to myself. It might have looked just like a normal entrance, but something seemed off about it. It was coming closer! But when I looked down, I saw that I was moving towards it. Pulled in like a helpless fish on a hook. The closer I got to that hole in the wall, the louder I could hear it– a deep bassline. I couldn't see inside, it was just black. Then suddenly, right in front of it, I was stuck in my tracks. I couldn't move anywhere. For the very first time I felt terrified.

From the deafening buzz, a voice appeared. I had to focus to hear it more clearly.

"Prepare, for soon it is time", I heard. I wanted to talk, but I was paralysed.

"Prepare, for soon it is time", I heard again.

A heavy weight filled my body. My feet were cold. I was touching the ground! I was struggling to stand and quickly the growing weight brought me to my knees, as if crushing me. Then in a moment of stillness I felt an intense burn run through my back. I was screaming in agony, but all I could do, was squeeze my right hand.

The burn went deeper and down towards my hips, till I saw one of my wings drop beside me. Then the other. The searing pain kept me from realising that I just lost my wings. Then all of a sudden, my paralysis left me and I dropped to the ground finally in control of my movements. It was then that I saw a figure behind me. A grey angel with double set of wings. In its hand was a scythe, which was covered in my blood and gave out a minor dust cloud.

"Forgive me sibling," it said, now in a much clearer tone. I couldn't respond. I was stunned. I never knew there were more like me. When I finally looked at its eyes, I saw that it was crying. And as it turned its back on me, the pain became so unbearable that darkness befell me.

I woke up in my pool of blood. I couldn't see it, but I could taste it. I couldn't see anything. As if someone shut off my eyes. I swiped my hands over the stone floor to push myself up, but my fingernail caught a small pebble. It was a weird feeling; I wouldn't have thought stone to be so rough. Hard yes, but not that rough. I tried to hurl myself on my knees, but fell on the wall, leaning against it. With the help of that trusty wall,

I could get on my feet. I was sweating and breathing heavily. As I stood there with both my arms on the wall, my back didn't hurt as much anymore. "What is going on?" I thought. "Who was that angel and why did it do that to me. Well… at least Lisa is safe. Lisa! Where is she? I need to find her!"

With that objective in mind, I twisted my torso to turn around, but I felt as if my back was opening up. It took my breath away, and I tensed up all over.

I didn't want to do that again and thought that as long as I don't turn my upper body in any way, it wouldn't be as painful. As stiff as a tree trunk I made my way across the basement, one little step after the other. I was lucky that I could remember the layout of the basement from when I came in.

Reaching the stairs that led up to the door felt like an incredible achievement. For that I celebrated by giving myself a short break. How on earth will I search for Lisa, let alone find her? I would have to crawl back home by the looks of it, but for now I wanted to concentrate on the next goal: to get out of this basement. With my left hand on the wall, I lifted my right knee in a ninety-degree angle and slowly planted it on the first step. With a swift push of the leg, I made it. I did that again, and again, and again, until I found myself standing in front of the door. Victory! I sighed in relief.

When I found the door handle, and held it tightly for support, the door swung open violently. It knocked me back and I fell down the stairs, nearly reaching the bottom.

"I will go down to get your bike. Okay?" I heard Tony say. Suddenly everything went white. Again, I couldn't see anything, but to my relief, different colours and shades slowly returned to me. He walked down the stairs swiftly, stepping through my body. As he grabbed a small, pink bicycle, I saw Marta standing on top of the stairs. She looked directly at me. I didn't know what I was supposed to do, so I just waved, not realising that my palm was still covered in blood.

Tony carried the bike up the stairs. "Daddy, who is in the basement?" Marta said.

"There is no one honey." Tony shrugged it off, shutting the door behind him.

I heard them have the same conversation that Lisa had multiple times during her childhood. About monsters, and closets, and beds, and darkness. I couldn't appreciate that thought though, because my back was literally killing me. I stood up with difficulty and went up those stupid stairs. I opened the door cautiously and closed it behind me. Alas! I made it. Across the living room I could see that it was a beautiful day. The sun was peeking through the blinds. How long was I gone for? I saw that the back door was cracked open.

"Hold on the handlebars. Don't let go. Do you understand?" I heard Tony's instruction in the background.

I was in their garden. When I stepped out, I was startled. I felt the sun on my skin. It felt striking, but warm. And the grass! The way it tickled my ankles while I walked through it, made the small trip around the house quite amusing.

When I reached the street, I saw Marta and Tony riding up and down it. One of the neighbours was grilling some meat, while the other sat on a plastic garden chair enjoying the sun.

It took me hours to reach Lisa's house. Till then the sun had set, and a cold current of winds swam through the streets. Shivering, I reached to the door, but it was closed. Of course, it was! Lisa never left the door open, afraid of intruders. Funny how I became the intruder. I looked through the window but couldn't see her. The living room lights were on though. I sat down on the stairs of the porch and waited. My stomach made noises and my nose was all stuffed. That was annoying.

I was constantly thinking about food. I dreamed to eat something. It was odd, because I never ate anything before. I was craving potatoes. Roasted, served with garlic butter and steamed vegetables. It was the same dish Lisa always made herself. It was not the fanciest of meals, but it was one of her 'weird-craving' dishes. Well, now I wanted some too.

Hours have passed, and I was still sitting on the porch. The streets were quite creepy during the night. I saw homeless people drag their feet forwards, passing me in a slow pace. Quite like me. Sad to think that they shuffle around from one place to another, never reaching their home. In this very moment I was homeless too. I had a place that I could call *home*, but what good was it when I didn't have the keys. Apart from the homeless, I saw the drunk. Some were both, drunk and homeless that is, but there were two boys returning from a party. I could smell the pungent odour. It made me squint. That must have been the famous alcohol. They came around the corner, laughing and walking in a zig-zag fashion. It was amazing how they weren't fazed by the cold. But a few steps behind them, from the corner appeared two *Buralag*. One of them was small and skinny, but the other was very similar to Lisa's. It was massive and hideous. They both saw me, laughed, and continued preying on these little boys. These demons prefer the young, they can squeeze more life out of them than the old. But once they take hold, they come back for more.

For a long time, nothing happened. Just the wind blew past, howling, blowing plastic bags onto sidewalks, and swinging the street cables around.

An hour or so before dawn, I saw a raccoon search the large garbage containers for food. When Lisa's garbage was on the menu, the raccoon noticed me sitting there. Instead of going for the food, it went onto the sidewalk, and sat down, right across from me. We were completely still. It looked right at me.

17

It made me think. How on earth did I end up like this? I thought about the angel once more. It was so beautiful. I wished I could be so magnificent. Yes, it cut off my wings, but I wouldn't have used them for long anyway, they were rotting away. What I didn't expect was to lose all my powers. And what did it mean by "Forgive me sibling". I never met that angel before, and apparently, we were family. I was curious how much more of my family I hadn't met. Also, what did it mean by "it's time". I pondered a long while, even though somewhere deep down I knew what it meant.

The thoughts during my wait made me oblivious to the fact that the cold numbed my back. I couldn't feel it anymore. To be entirely honest I couldn't feel anything at all.

When I took notice of my surroundings, I saw that the raccoon was gone. I was left entirely on my own again.

The warm sunlight woke me up. I couldn't remember falling asleep. I must've been exhausted. I stood up carefully and peeked in the window again. Lisa was in there, watching TV on her reclining chair. How long would I have to wait for her to open this damn door. I watched intently at her, trying to persuade her to come open the door. In my morning grogginess I forgot that she couldn't hear me. I had enough of waiting, so I used the opportunity to tap the window. Of all people she could be the one who could hear me. But nothing. I picked up rocks, maybe she could *see* that. But also, nothing. I didn't understand. I was able to open doors, touch walls and walk on the ground, but they aren't able to see when I am moving objects around them. What was happening?

I slammed my fist through the window in frustration, shattering it in a blast. The shards flew everywhere. I screamed because I broke two knuckles. Another look at Lisa confirmed my fear. She didn't react.

I climbed through the window. The pain was agonising. The flesh in my back ripped anew. I was stumbling through the kitchen to walk into the living room.

Finally, I was with her.

Holding my busted hand tightly, I gently sat down opposite her on a leather couch. A trail of small blood drops followed me to the couch. But that didn't matter. I got lost in my pain.

"Lisa, I am sorry," my vision was blurred and wet. "Run, please, just run. You won't be able to escape, but at least you will hope that you can. If only you could see me. *I* need you right now." I gently stretched over the coffee table, took the vase and used its water to wash my face and hands. The water ran through my scars, penetrated deep, perhaps cleansing me.

"But of course, you wouldn't know. You'd never care. I saw you do things you shouldn't have done. I protected you from things that you probably deserved. I made you avoid tragedies. But now I am the tragedy!" I stood up hastily. "Look at me!" I shouted. "Lisa! Look at me!"

As I stood over her, she stood up and stepped right through me. She opened the very window I smashed. She scratched a bit of dirt off the windowpane with her fingernails and took a bottle of beer from the fridge.

Still fuelled with rage, I stomped to the fridge myself, stepping all over the broken shards on the floor. I ate all the leftovers, because as I took a nibble from a cheese slice, there was no stopping me. With it I drank one bottle of beer, then another. Then I emptied a bottle of wine that stood on the kitchen counter.

Quickly everything became hazy, and I fell over face first. I crawled to the bathroom. I wasn't sure why.

After a lapse of memory, I saw my head hovering over the toilet bowl, which was filled with vomit. While I was holding the toilet seat, I felt glass shards penetrate deeper into my skin. Weirdly enough there was no pain to be felt, I just felt things move *inside* my hand.

I pushed my weight to the sink and pulled myself up. Now leaning against the sink, I saw water droplets in the sink. I must have used it. When I swung my head up, I saw the mirror, and I began to cry.

Another lapse of memory saw me in the garden, panting hard. I was in the middle of her neglected garden, filled with wild bushes and tall grass and weeds. The thorns of a bush beside me caught my hair. My back was on fire. My tears dried on my cheeks, leaving a crusty feeling behind. A headache rang all my alarms. I was ashamed and embarrassed by how I had let myself go. I never knew how you could be angry at someone you loved so much. I had done just that. I didn't enjoy thinking about it, but at the time it just felt so good.

It took me forever to get out of the bushes cautiously and enter the house again. This time I just entered through the back door, the lock was broken. The door squeaked and cracked when I opened it. I saw cushions ripped apart, the couches scratched and partly ripped. The table was flipped. The ceiling lamp was not a ceiling lamp anymore. The TV laid flat on the ground, and bits of vomit covered part of the carpet. All that must've been me. That would explain all my bruises and sick stomach.

It stunk all over, from the vomit. It was acidic and pungent. I found Lisa asleep in her armchair, hanging her head outward like a lifeless doll. The same armchair was buried in the porch, under wooden planks that it penetrated. All I wanted to do was to go to sleep. I felt dead. I threw a blanket around me that hung over a cupboard. It would have been much more comfortable if it wasn't wet.

Lisa's phone rang, but she didn't wake up. I rushed in little steps and tried to grab her phone, but I slammed my hand onto the table, right through the phone. Before the screen went dark, I glimpsed at the date and time: "4.23 pm, Thursday".

"WHAAT?" I gasped. "That can't be right," I said to myself. "Where was I the last couple days?"

Talking to myself became a quick habit. I didn't have anyone to talk to. I never had the urge to talk, but words began to just flow right out.

"How long was I unconscious in that basement for? Where was Lisa, and what did I miss?" I stopped talking, because I got overwhelmed by the sheer number of thoughts and questions raging in my head. It didn't help the headache.

"Just calm down." Saying that didn't help. I was always confused by why people said that all the time. Phrases like "don't think about it" or "calm down" never worked. Quite ironic that *I* have now said that. Maybe that was a normal reaction. I was quite angry at myself for proving myself to be a hypocrite though.

I scratched my head. But my thoughts were interrupted by quick visions that whizzed by. They were real, yet imaginary. My hands shivered and my breath became much more erratic. I leaned over the table. Then everything went still.

The fridge stopped buzzing, the clock didn't tick anymore. I couldn't hear the birdsong outside. Time had stopped again, just like in the park back then. Suddenly all the glass shards faded. The scratches on the wall disappeared and the furniture returned to its original place. At the same time the outdoors started to blacken, until the house hovered in complete darkness. Lisa was still sleeping, I ran to her to shake her.

"Wake up!" I said. She wasn't sleeping, she too was frozen.

Through the gaps in the doors and windows, through the floor and ceiling came a black mist. It gathered right next to the fridge. In an unthinking reaction I somehow grabbed Lisa's phone and threw it at the mist. I was astonished to how I could touch the phone then. It passed right through the Buralag and crashed against the tiles of the kitchen wall.

"Step away from her," the mist said, forming into a huge figure.

"Over my dead body!" I yelled, grabbing a cup from the table and the vase.

The Buralag smiled back at me, mocking my weak appearance by peering through the mist.

"You're already dead."

It approached Lisa, whose heart had stopped.

"No!" I threw the cup. "No, No, No! Get away from her."

But just like so many things, it had passed right through me. Pure evil had passed me, I was blinded by the dark mist that the Buralag was formed from. As it cleared, I saw the same grey angel standing there before me, with its arms wide open.

"I'm so sorry my dear," the angel spoke. But I didn't care. I turned to the Buralag again and piled my fists through its body, swearing profusely at it.

The grey angel hugged me from behind, locking my arms in it. "Don't make it harder for yourself," it said. "Breathe slowly. In, and out."

"Just kill me!" I ignored the angel's instructions. "You are taking her away from me! Not like this."

Its hug squeezed me tighter.

"Let go. Let her go."

As it said that, I felt my rage extinguish in me. My fists opened up, and my head sank a bit. The hug loosened and I turned around to face the angel. Again, I was baffled by its face.

Its hair was longer than mine. The angel looked youthful, but its eyes were a pit of sorrow. They were filled with wisdom.

"How?" I asked.

The angel hugged me again, while tears poured down my face.

"Just like that." It said. "Just like that…"

Rather than overflowing with thoughts, my mind turned blank and I thought of nothing. Lisa had died, and it felt as if I did too.

Not long after I'd imagine, I opened my eyes again and I was standing inside this nothingness – a whiteness even without a floor to stand on. The grey angel had disappeared. I felt good. While I was scanning my body, I didn't recognise myself. I was startled. When I jumped back, my wings violently opened up. I had my wings back! With all their feathers too!

From the whiteness in front of me, I noticed Lisa come towards me. She didn't see me yet, and walked aimlessly in confusion.

I flew to her. "Lisa," I said. When she saw me, she stopped in her tracks and stared at me in awe and fear.

"Don't be afraid Lisa," I landed on my feet. I was unexpectedly calm. Everything was clear and I had forgotten what had happened not too long ago.

"Where am I? And who the hell are you?" Lisa said.

"Don't worry about where we are. It doesn't matter. What matters is where we will be going." I didn't answer her second question, because she already knew who I was.

"Is this real?" She looked around frantically, perhaps for any other people. I guess I freaked her out.

While she was looking around, I came to her and offered her my hand. "Come with me." She looked back at me and held my hand, however I could tell she didn't fully trust me. That was okay.

When our hands met, the whiteness around us transformed into highlands. All around us steep cliffs and mountain peaks. In the distance we could see a flock of sheep, bouncing happily across the grass. There were a few clouds, that every now and then offered us a pause from the sun. We began to walk across the fields. She held my hand tightly.

"Beautiful, isn't it?" I began talking. "I love the mountains just as much as you do. What I love most is the isolation. It is totally silent. Can you hear that?" I stopped and looked at her for a moment. "Nothing but the breeze," I continued. "Everything is so far away as well. You can see what you are walking towards, but it doesn't seem to get any closer, until you stand just in front of it. Then when you turn around and see from where you came from... it is just amazing."

Lisa stopped, dropping her head. She started sobbing. As I turned to her, she spoke, "My kids! T-they are all alone now. I left them! And - and my mother! What kind of daughter am I?"

Her legs gave way and she plummeted onto her knees. I kneeled too on the soft grass, embracing her tightly, so she would not have to fall any further. And as she cried in despair and desperation, I felt it too. Her love towards her family flowed right into me, along with all the confusion, fear, and disappointment. This was the first time I could hug her, and I felt so grateful for that. But as my head rested on her shoulders, I could see the grey angel in the distance.

"Let them go," I said, hoping it might work for her as well. "Just let it all go, Lisa."

All of a sudden, I felt a massive wave of negativity and sorrow burst into me. While I squinted, trying to get over that pain, Lisa rose to her feet again. She took a deep breath.

It took me a few moments to pull myself together, and when I did, we walked together towards a gentle hill.

We talked the entire way, I answered her questions, she answered mine. We told jokes and reminisced over our experiences.

At the top of this seemingly forever-going hill, we finally stopped. A massive lake that we looked down on silenced our witty conversation. Engulfed by mountains and fields, a shadow was cast upon it. And yet, the water twinkled, and flowers bloomed. Wild horses galloped along the edges of the lake under a soaring flock of seagulls, whose squawks echoed in the valley.

Somehow, I just knew what I had to do. "Lisa?" I asked. "Can I carry you?"

Without a word or hesitation, she came closer and I lifted her and flew beyond the steep cliffs towards the water. As we came closer to the beach, something seemed off. Just before landing, Lisa said "Coins?". Yes, she was right! The whole beach made out of small coins, which felt cold when I landed.

"Well… that is a surprise," Lisa said, taking one into her hand. "They are blank, look." The one that I held had a rough edge and was slightly bent. I attempted to straighten it, but that seemed impossible, so I threw it towards the lake, as far as I could, out of slight frustration. But as it hit the water, it did not produce any waves. It hit the water, tumbling and rolling on the surface. Lisa saw it and threw another onto the water – same result.

"What the – ," she murmured puzzlingly. Completely intrigued now, she slowly took a step towards the water. Her foot sunk.

"W-what is happening?" she asked me.

"Hmmm, I'm not sure. But better stay out of the water, God knows what is in there." As I said that, she jumped back hastily.

"You try," she said.

I didn't really want to. I was scared of the water. I knew it was pathetic, but it was the truth. Of course I had to do it, what would she think if her guardian angel told her that they were frightened.

So, I took my step… and just as I was supposed to hit the water, my heel struck a hard, yet invisible surface.

"Hey! How are you doing it?" she exclaimed laughingly. "I also want to!"

I was relieved I didn't actually have to touch the water. I took another step, and then another, and another. I was walking on water.

"Lisa, look at me!" I stuttered.

"Yes, absolutely incredible. I will give it another go."

I watched her as her following attempt failed. She sighed in disappointment.

I came to her and offered my hand, "If I may."

"It doesn't matter anymore. I can't do it."

"No, you can't, we saw that twice," I laughed, as she frowned at me. "But perhaps we can do it together?"

When she gave it another go, this time holding my hand, she made it.

"Look! Look! Oh my Go-," she caught herself. "-Gosh. Oh my gosh…"

That was funny. As if I didn't hear her cursing before. So cute of her to cut her bad habits in my presence.

So, we stood there for a while. She looked around to see what was under her. It was more coins and some rocks. But eventually we walked further and further into the lake until we found a bench, which stood on the water on which a person was sitting. He was admiring a small tree sapling that grew out the water just in front of him.

"Who is that?" she asked.

"I don't know, but let's see."

Again, came the feeling of complete understanding and peacefulness. This feeling never lasted long, but it felt so right, nearly as if I was certain of the immediate future and being completely satisfied with it.

When we came closer, we heard the person on the bench say: "Took you a while, my pumpkin."

And as soon as we heard it, Lisa stopped in her tracks.

"Dad?" she cried out loud. "Dad?" she let go of me and ran towards him. The moment she let my hand go, I started sinking into the water.

The man stood up from the bench and caught his daughter in a tight hug.

"Oh, my Lisa!"

"I cannot believe it dad. It's really you. I –"

That is all I could hear, until the water swallowed me, and I vanished into the depths.

It all happened so quickly, all I could muster was a scream, which was muted by the deep, and erratic movements, which were humbled by the swallowing darkness of the lake. But at least Lisa was safe. That was all that really mattered.

Chapter Two

Nothingness. That was what I saw, what I heard, what I felt... what I was. Until there was light. A rude awakening, with an acute headache and a rush of air invading me. The silence broke by a loud clattering and a rhythmic whistling.

I raised my head, noticing that I was lying down.

"Ah! I wondered when you would finally come back."

Who was that? And where was that that I needed to 'come back' from? I opened my eyes to see myself cooking in the sun, lying on the coins next to the lake. That was a relief, to know where I was. Then the loud clattering continued. I turned to see what the annoying noise was made by.

A woman in a flannel dress collected the coins in a bucket. She didn't seem to feel bad about the jarring noise. Then she took the bucket into her arms and shook it hard.

"Can you stop!?" I shouted. My headache was continuing to kill me, and she just made it worse, seemingly on purpose.

"A bit of a wakeup call won't hurt," she said. "Don't be such a baby and stand up."

"Who are you anyway, and what are we doing *here?*" I said standing up, brushing myself off and inspecting the state of my wings.

"You're fine. I pulled you out of the water. Seemed like you needed help."

"How did you know I was in the water?"

"I heard you. No one would miss that high-pitched scream."

"Very funny…" I turned to the water to see if I could see the bench. 'Where are you?' I thought to myself.

"She has gone beyond," the woman answered. "She is lucky, her dad is an amazing guy." Perplexed that she just heard my thoughts, I wanted to confront her about it, but she cut me off.

"One doesn't have to be a psychic, it's practically written on your face."

"What?"

"You are looking for her," she said.

"Do you know where she went?"

She didn't answer me and kept looking at the coins, reaching down for one. She went over it with her fingers and put the one gently in the bucket. Watching her made me ponder whether I knew her. She seemed so… familiar.

"Do I know you?" I asked impulsively.

She grinned. "Yes, I think you heard of me, but I know *you* much better." She put down her bucket and came closer to me. "What's the matter my dear Kasbiele?".

My name! I hadn't heard my name for so long. So long, in fact that I forgot I had one. Hang on, that must mean…

"Yes, it's me. How are you now?" she asked.

"I am so sorry! Please forgive me."

"I *don't* forgive you, because there is nothing to forgive you for," she said.

"Are you sure?"

"If I wasn't always sure then that would be a rollercoaster, wouldn't it?" She's got a point to be fair. "Now tell me, what got you so troubled?"

"Troubled? I am not troubled."

"Are you not. Then why do you seek for Lisa here?"

"I want to make sure she's safe," I said.

"Ah, so not even my own home is safe enough for you now?" she said with a smile. "All this beauty around, all this I've created for you, and I'm still not worthy of your trust."

"Then why won't you just tell me whether Lisa is alright?" I asked frustrated.

"Because I know that this is not the question you really want ask. Tell me child; What is it you really seek to know?"

I wasn't used to talking to someone all-knowing. For a second it creeped me out to know that she sees me in my entirety – my thoughts, my feelings, my questions, my frustrations, my goals. She will even know exactly what I am thinking right now, these very words.

"So?" she caught me at my break.

"I'm lost," I said. "I have tried so hard for Lisa, but in the end it wasn't enough. I have done everything for her, but it all ended in suffering." I clasped my hand and turned towards the lake once more. "I tried my best, and failed... She died because I couldn't save her."

My hands started to shake, and tears welled up in my eyes. The woman appeared in front of me once more and wiped my falling tears off my cheek.

"Could I have saved her if I was better?" I asked.

"Oh, my child, how far you have come. You really are as loving as I hoped you'd become, but life on earth has scarred you, hasn't it?" She caressed my wings. "Some things were just meant to happen, that even you couldn't have changed... or shouldn't."

"What do you mean?"

She grabbed me by my shoulders and turned me around. In that instance our surroundings changed. We were placed in an old village surrounded by fields and cattle. Small huts sparsely placed around a little well. It was a sunny day, but windy.

The woman, who stood now next to me, pointed at a man sitting on a tiny wooden stool milking one of the few cows in the area. He was dressed in a long garment, which picked up even the slightest breeze.

"This is Nikolaos," she said. "An honest man who lived long ago in this small village. He was a gift to the community, as he was kind and generous without fail. An amazing father of five, and a caring husband."

As she said that, the visions of his past in front of us showed exactly what she was describing, scenes of laughter and joy, scenes of humility and care. Through the visions, I could see his whole life history, the good, as well as the bad.

"But as everything, there had to be an end. When he grew old and weak, this day that you see before you was his time to die."

While Nikolaos was milking his cow, men on horseback with torches appeared from the hills. I counted 13 of them, all of whom were galloping towards the little huts. Women and children rushed into the buildings, while the men of the village huddled together, each of them carrying a tool: hammers, hoes, and knives. Nikolaos led his cow to a nearby shelter and joined the men.

The horsemen split and surrounded the village. All of them but one began setting the huts ablaze. The people in them ran out to the men.

"Now that you are all here," said one rider who looked to be the leader, "We demand you give up all your valuables *at once.*"

After a moment of silence Nikolaos took it upon himself to represent the village.

"We are poor and few. We have nothing to spare," Nikolaos said spreading his arms wide. "However, all you see around you is all we would give, for the price of mercy."

"I will not speak to armed farmers. How dare you ask for mercy when you hold weapons yourself? Surrender your weapons to us and we will do as we see fit."

"No," a man holding a scythe stepped out of the huddle. "How can we trust you, the ones who burn our lives to ashes!"

The lead rider whistled, signalling to another rider who shortly thereafter kicked the man in the back, making him fall onto the ground together with the scythe.

"Pick it up and hand it to me," the leader ordered Nikolaos, which was followed without hesitation. "What a wonderful tool… to be able to reap fruits with one swing," he inspected the old and rusted scythe.

The woman in the flannel dress next to me clapped her hands together. Then, not only could I see the farmers and riders, but also each of their angels. They were scattered all around, drowned by swarms of demons that tried to reach the men, women, and children. The angels of the riders were tied in shackles, being pulled by the horses.

"We didn't come all this way to leave empty-handed," the leader continued.

"Take all you want," Nikolaos said.

"Alright then," the rider responded by shouting some quick commands to the others on horseback. They began killing all livestock around, that were already frantic due to the growing fires. It didn't take long, as the village had only a few animals.

The villagers watched on as all their livelihood was destroyed. But they didn't say anything.

"We will come back once the sun has hidden behind the horizon. Gather all your valuables together for us to collect. If not, then today shall be your last day breathing," the leader turned, so that Nikolaos was at his side. "This is for your defiance..."

A demon, bloodthirsty and insane, headed straight to Nikolaos. At the same time, the leader swung the scythe towards Nikolaos. He was left undefended.

His angel flew as fast it could to Nikolaos. The flap of its mighty wings was so full of desperation and haste that it created a whirlwind behind it. Just as the scythe should have penetrated his neck, the angel flew into Nikolaos.

The swing was successful, but the rider remained stunned to see Nikolaos stand in front of him without any sign of hurt.

Nikolaos' angel lay next to him, drowning in its blood, because the scythe had cut its wings clean off.

It died shortly after.

"The rider was supposed to kill him," the woman in the flannel dress explained. "His angel loved him so much, that it betrayed Nikolaos' fate. It was the first time an angel had interfered with death. A love so strong that I haven't seen before."

"But isn't it good?" I asked.

"See for yourself."

We saw Nikolaos in the future; an old man barely able to walk and very sick. He was in an agora selling a bag of fruits he was barely able to carry. Upon reaching down to pick up a handful of fruits that a customer had just paid for, he stumbled and fell onto the stone floor headfirst. He died.

His angel waited for him in the same whiteness I found myself in, meeting Lisa for the first time. The angel looked for Nikolaos, knowing he had died, but he was nowhere to be found.

"Nikolaos!" the angel exclaimed. "Nikolaos!"

The woman turned to me and said, "His soul was stuck in his body, for he lived a portion of his life without an angel, and so died alone too."

"What happened with him?"

"Well, unwilling to let his soul forever longing peace, I changed the angel's fate. Just like it did."

We saw how the angel grew more rattled and confused. It flew back and forth trying to find Nikolaos, but at the end of his search, he had found the same scythe that once nearly took Nikolaos' life.

"Azrael," a deep voice filled the white void, "you have saved Nikolaos from his fate that this weapon should have sealed. Now the weapon is yours."

Azrael, spooked by the voice, did as instructed and picked up the scythe. Upon its touch, the scythe gave out a dark mist, embedding Azreal in it.

"Now you have the power to defy men and your kin. I allow you to bring Nikolaos home, but in doing so, you will be the guardian of all the dead," the voice trembled the void again.

Out of the dark mist, Azrael emerged grey and with two pairs of wings.

"I have given you the foresight of death. With it I task you to make angels powerless when the time comes. You are chosen to be the angel of death."

"This is how it all happened," the woman said, and the visions faded, leaving me staring at the lake once more.

"I still have so many questions," I said.

"I know Kasbiele," she said stretching her hand out. "You need to leave it here I'm afraid."

"Leave what?" I was confused. I felt something in my hand. It was a coin, shiny and new with Lisa's head engraved on it. I surrendered it onto her open palm.

"Everyone has to leave their riches behind in order to move forward." She put the coin in her bucket.

"I still don't know whether I was any good for her. She went through so much that wasn't her fault. Is it *my* fault perhaps?"

"Kasbiele," she said hugging me, "the world is ruled by desires of men. For you to understand that, you have to see as they see. You need to feel like they feel."

She began shaking the bucket filled with coins. The clattering was deafening this time, but amidst the noise I could faintly hear her say, "Farewell, my dear Kale." Then, after a blink of an eye I found myself kneeling before a baby violently shaking a toy rattle.

"Kale, honey, I'm home." A door shut and keys were thrown into a metal bowl. "Everything alright?" A woman came and took the baby in her arms. Her brown hair that grazed my face smelled like something I never smelled before. "Kale, thank you for looking out after Ada. I know she can be a handful sometimes, but I think it would be good for you to spend some time with your sister."

My sister? I have a sister? Is she my mother now? My confusion worsened the headache even more. I don't know why but I touched my forehead and it was very warm.

"Oh no, do you have a headache honey?"

I nodded.

I felt her hand now caress my forehead, "You are burning up! To bed with you *now*." And just like that I saw myself going up some stairs into a room covered in clothes and the smell of crisps. When I lay in bed, I felt a great relief. My walls were covered in posters of people playing football, wearing high socks and shirts in the same colour. They were sweating too.

After my thoughts died down, all I could hear was a faint ticking that seemed to come from the clock on the wall. After some time, the woman came in with a tray in her hand with a bowl on it.

"Thought about cleaning all this up? After you get better you should get to it. But now just eat your soup and try to get better."

"Thank you," I said.

Alone the steam that covered my face, felt so good, so warm. And the smell! Woah, so good.

"If you need anything, let me know. I need to go back take care of Ada. Thanks again honey," a kiss on my cheek ended her short stay.

What the hell just happened? Where am I? Who am I? And again, like so often before, questions plagued my mind. I am accustomed to not get answers, but this concerned me, and I just *must* know. So, I stood up and went to my desk. It had an open notebook on it with pencils and pens scattered all around. The notebook had all sorts of numbers, lines, and scribble on it. The cover said:

Mathematics
Kale Josef Ingram
6th Grade

I have heard about Mathematics. It always interested me how people try to quantise their world around them. Back when I saw Lisa learn relentlessly for tests and homework, I learned with her. Lisa, how much I miss her. She seems so far away now.

At the side of the desk I could see a picture of a young boy, a girl, a baby and two parents posing for the family photo. I thought about that kid that looked at me on the picture. He was now me, or rather I became him. I thought about that for the rest of the day, while eating the delicious soup, inspecting the posters more closely, and lying in bed in the comfort of a heavy duvet.

I open my eyes and I feel incredibly tired. The sun hit my face, through a gap in the curtains. What just happened? It was just dark. My movements weren't sharp, and my thoughts drifted so heavily, I thought I was poisoned. When I rolled to one side of the bed, my head hit a cold patch on the pillow. So satisfying.

During my next thought I realised I had my eyes shut again. So, I decided to just hurl myself up in a moment of drive. My face felt dry, my breath stank, and my hair resembled a bird's nest. A sudden pressure in my stomach area, made me highly uncomfortable. But just in time I figured that I needed to go to the toilet. Oh boy did it feel good.

Now I can finally understand why Lisa had to go to the toilet every time she woke up. It would be difficult to continue with that pain. I flushed, and walked up to the sink to wash my hands. "Aaah!" I shrieked loudly, and fell back onto the floor. Now I really woke up. I stood up and saw myself in the mirror. I had brown eyes and dark hair. I had what Lisa called 'little shits' on my face - red dots on my cheeks, and quite a lot of them actually. It was so fascinating; I am actually a person! ...*I am a person.*

Then suddenly, like a flash, I knew my mum and dad. As if a dam opened up and all memories reached me. I knew all kinds of things. My dad works in IT and loves boardgames. My mum, an incredible baker, works part-time as a gardener for the government. I have an older sister, Marcelina, that plays volleyball and just began high school. My birthday is June 23.

After that weird moment, I brushed my teeth for the very first time. My gums were bleeding – I hope I did it right.

"Good morning sleepy head!" I heard my mum say. "Feeling better?"

"Yes mum."

"Good to hear. Come down, I made breakfast."

Wow, my first breakfast! I was so excited that I rushed changing clothes and ran down, nearly falling. Still getting used to stairs.

"You will be wearing that?" my sister said mockingly. "Man, you really are getting old quick."

"Hey! Leave Kale alone. He can dress how he likes." My mother defended me. "Just eat your bagels."

Bagels, never had those. Neither have I tried, tomatoes, cucumber, jam, toast, cheese, ham, carrots, orange juice... I will try everything! I first took a bagel from a small basket and attempted to cut it in half.

"So how did you sleep?" My mother asked me.

"Amazing! I closed my eyes and when I opened them it was bright again. Felt quite weird."

Marcelina burst out laughing, spitting partly chewed bagel on her plate.

"No need to be sarcastic. I see you are still not in the best of moods. Anyway, are you excited for church tomorrow? It will be the first Mass of our new priest. I think it is important to give him a warm welcome."

Church? I haven't been there for a very long time! I wonder what it's like.

"Yes mum, I *am* excited. Are we all going?" I answered her. My sister looked at me with fear in her eyes. My mother seemed to be quite surprised by the question.

"I would be very happy if we would, but you know exactly how your father and Marcelina feel about church... Do you need a hand with that bagel?" My sister grinned in response to my mother and kept eating. My mum grabbed my bagel out of my hands and cut it best she could. I squished and twisted the bagel in my hand. It was quite challenging to cut a soft thing I noticed. I was glad mum helped me.

"Don't help him. Kale is not a baby anymore." I heard my dad say. He had a deep voice and was taller than expected as he emerged from the back with a cardboard box in his hand.

I was shocked to see an angel pass through the wall into the living room behind my dad. I screamed and so scared everyone there. I even woke up Ada, who started to cry upstairs.

"Kale!" Marcelina cried out loud.

I couldn't respond, as I locked eyes with the utter beauty of the angel. The angel felt uneasy, possibly scared. "I can see you," I whispered. It quickly turned around and escaped through the wall. The little piece of silence broke.

"Stop playing around Kale. Stop being stupid for once." I heard Marcelina say.

"I'm sorry," I dropped my head.

"It wasn't at all funny. Look at what you did." My mother was on the floor picking up pieces of eggshells. "Bring more paper towel! I-it's not a tragedy, only three broke."

My dad came back swiftly with the towels. I should have helped, as I was the one that caused the mess, but all I could think of was the angel. Where did it come from? It was like seeing myself in the mirror for the second time. But *gosh* was it

39

beautiful. Its wings, so proportional and strong – mine weren't. I couldn't stop thinking about it.

It took me a while to finish my breakfast. I learned that tomatoes were disgusting, and that cheese was heavenly. But on a bagel, I preferred chocolate spread. Because of that 'mishap', my dad told me I had to help him with mowing the lawn. It wasn't my favourite thing to do – standing in one place pulling and releasing the electric cord so it wasn't in the way of the mower. I was happy though to have made my dad's job easier.

Time passed very quickly. It seemed that I just finished breakfast, and now there was lunch on the table. I was hungry, yes, but experiencing the speed of an ordinary day was confusing. After lunch, my dad passed out on the couch with a funny snore, and my sister ran back to her room. I didn't really know what to do. I thought about Lisa, and it gave me an idea. I went to the living room and attempted to turn on the TV. And as soon as I held the remote in my hand, a flash sparked again. Suddenly I knew what channels I liked, how the remote worked, and at what times my favourite show ran. Naturally, I put it on, but it was just a re-run.

"Can't wait for Wednesday *ha*?" Mum said. I turned to see her behind a big PC monitor across the room.

"Yeah, I guess. The re-run is better than nothing," I said. It was all so obvious now. The characters 'Ben', 'Tommy', and 'George', go on these insane adventures together. And the intro song of the show was so catchy. I sang, "Across the land of inventors and the kind, we see the boys running to adventures far and wide… "

The next time I looked at the clock, I saw three hours have passed. I forced myself to get off the couch, which was tougher than it should've been, and went to my room. On the way there I could hear Marcelina sing wholeheartedly through her door. I stopped for a while, as it was quite nice to listen to. 'I should complement her' I thought to myself. But as soon as I opened her door:

"Get out!" She came heavy-footed and slammed the door into me. Well… I figured she didn't need compliments.

I wasn't sure what to do in my room. I tried to see what sort of things were in my room. There was a shelf with books on it. I took a glance, but whenever I opened a book, I knew the plot. Fantasy was the most common genre, with incredibly strong heroes fighting some kind of villain. It wasn't long till I was distracted by an urge. Something was missing, but I couldn't quite figure it out. It wasn't the books, and neither was it in the toy box I found under my bed. It wasn't the figurines either that stood glued together and partly painted on the desk. The urge grew restless, but as soon as I opened my nightstand, with a rush of relief I found what gave me some peace – my phone. I unlocked it by somehow remembering my passcode. All the apps reminded me of Lisa again, and the long times she spent on her phone. That, as well as the re-appearing flashes of memories, helped me to navigate through it, understanding who the names in my 'Contacts' were, and what all apps did.

I got a couple messages from Ben, my best friend. He needed help preparing for a test we had for Monday. Oh gosh! How could I miss it? I needed to get right on it.

I sat down and opened my books in panic. "G-Geo… Geography…" I mumbled. "paaaaaage 64". The book was filled with illustrations and annotations, which I had trouble remembering – Rivers didn't seem to be very exciting. It took me ages to learn about meanders, riverbeds, ox-bow lakes and so forth. But at least I was able to help Ben a bit with it. And just like that my first full day ended, after a brief dinner and tea of course. I was happy to go to bed too, as I was unexpectedly tired. Safe to say, I slept 'like a bear', Lisa's favourite catchphrase.

"Kale... Kale. Kale!" I heard. "Time to get up for church." I knew I was excited for it, but I would trade anything, even church, just to sleep longer. I never thought I would think such a thing. The only thing that made me get up was the thought of disappointing my mother.

After getting ready we took the car to get to church. It wasn't the same as flying, but felt good not needing to walk, especially seeing how far away the church was. On the way there we turned to some side streets and in front of one house there was an older lady waving at us. It was Grandma Ela! We pulled over to let her in.

"Ahh! How happy I am to see you! And you brought that little sucker as well!" Grandma Ela said.

My mum slapped her on the shoulder as soon as she sat in the front passenger seat. "Mum!"

"What? Kale, you know I'm just joking," Ela turned to me gifting me a wink and a firm rub on my knee. "If I knew you'd come along I would give you something more spectacular, but here you go."

She handed me a red lollipop. The brand was unfamiliar, and the packaging seemed cheap, but I was over the moon. There was always something magical with the sweets grandparents buy. I never saw them in stores, but they were always on the living room table when I visited them, next to China plates and probably a million pictures of family.

Having Grandma Ela around was amazing, that meant that I could talk to someone in the car who was a bit livelier. I didn't think my mother wasn't great, but she was a bit of a 'stick in the mud' sometimes. When we finally arrived and got out of the car, I saw so many people outside the church waiting for Mass to begin. Some were laughing loudly, others were smoking. But most of them were standing still, waiting. I guessed they liked the fresh air. We went straight inside, and to my surprise there were many more people inside. The church wasn't just a church, it was a cathedral! There were statues of saints and religious figures on the side. Everywhere I looked I saw patterns in colour of gold. The ceiling was marvellous too, so high up in fact, I couldn't quite make out its patterns and details. It was then that I realised that my eyesight for distant things wasn't sharp at all. But I couldn't miss the humongous cross behind the altar. It overshadowed the whole interior. To be honest, it made me a little uneasy. But soon enough, the people who waited outside finally came in and took the remainder of the free seats. It got very quiet. In that silence everybody stood up. I was too far to see but I heard the priest start the Mass.

I didn't know that church could be so boring. It didn't take long until I started yawning excessively. But I got stuck in and tried to focus. It was just about the most difficult thing; my eyes were so heavy. I opened them for a second or two, just for them to fall back close against my will. I forced them open again and shrieked just like during yesterday's breakfast. The priest stopped for a second, to see whether everything was alright. I could feel my mother shrink down in embarrassment as people sitting around us gave us the mad look.

I saw angels again. But this time, there were so many! They talked with one another, laughed, pointed at specific people in the crowd. Some of them stayed very close to their human. Never in my life did I see so many angels.

Then I remembered my life with Lisa. I wondered where all of them were back then! I thought I was the only one. Completely forgetting the Mass, I looked at each of the angels in silence, but in complete awe. All of them were different in their own way – beautiful in their own way. Even if I wanted to, I couldn't get my eyes off them. In the crowd I saw a few who were glowing. They weren't just happy, they looked content.

But at some specific point all of them were glowing at the same time for a short period of time – they were all content together, except for two.

One was very thin, sitting… cowering in the crowd. With its head dropped between its raised knees, you could tell it was staring into a void. It needed to be seen desperately, but it was alone. The other one I could relate to a lot. I could see that it had the same broken wings that I did. It was strong but covered in bruises and cuts. It looked uneasy, scanning around, looking for something. It had not yet accepted its fate - still not aware that one cannot change God's will. It reminded me of the trapped feeling I had. The time where my love for Lisa was the only thing I had, and I held on to it until it killed me. I wondered who it was that rejected that poor angel.

"- you stay at Ela's for that. What do you think?", my mother whispered to me.

"Hmm?"

"Do you want to visit Grandpa afterwards?" she repeated. "If you join me, I will drop you off at Ela's when we drive back." As she said that I saw my grandpa in quick visions. Then I knew what she meant.

"Yes, that would be wonderful." Grandma looked over to me and gave a quick thumbs up in response to me.

As I turned to face the altar, on which the priest stood, I found that the angels were gone, but I knew they were still there. When the Mass ended, everybody rushed to get out. The people's faces lit up. I wished to believe that they were grateful and happy to have sat in such a spiritual place, being forgiven of their sins. But I knew their minds were occupied by selfish desire – happy that it was 'finally over'. I wasn't proud that I belonged to them.

My mother sent me to the graveyard, while she went to the market on the other side of the road to buy some candles and flowers. Grandma Ela joined her. I had to go along a straight path by the side of the cathedral. It was empty, and the closer I got to the graveyard, the less I could hear the cheerful talk and the starting up of cars in front of the cathedral. At the entrance, the small gate was cracked open, and just by it stood a massive metal cross that greeted you. It was showered with flowers. Without hesitation I made my way to grandpa's grave.

The tall gravestones filled the horizon, but a faint light caught my eye. In the far distance there was a candle being lit. I wasn't alone! As Grandpa's grave was in the same area, I got closer and closer, and finally recognised an elderly man standing in front of an old grave. One candle was the only decoration it had. A set of trees blocked my view, and as I passed them, I saw that the man wasn't alone either. Leaning on the grave was the same thin angel that cowered in the cathedral. Its long hair hung from the edges of the stone; its wings buried into the dirt. I knew exactly what it was like, so I decided to go there and at least acknowledge them. I walked silently and stopped next to the old man. I glanced at the stone. Some of the engraved words were faded, but it said:

In loving memory

Mary Kristling

A mother full of heart &
the best wife in the world

The angel looked up, but not straight at me. Its eyes were cloudy, and a great scar covered its face. Its left arm looked lame, and the shoulder was dislocated. But despite its obvious pain, it gave out a smile.

45

"Hello there," the old man said, a little confused. "Can I help you with something?"

"My mother went to buy some candles and flowers. You're the only one here."

The old man clasped his hands together, "Who did you come to visit?"

"Grandpa, over there," I pointed.

"Ah, how nice of you to keep him in your memory. You for sure loved him a lot."

"I did... What about you? Who are you visiting?"

"My wife," he smirked. The angel then continued to lay on the gravestone but seemed to be in a better spirit than before. I thought about what to say. I put my hands in my jeans pockets to find the lollipop. I didn't have anything else I could've given, so I took it out and laid it on the stone.

"T-Thank you very much. She appreciates it for sure. In fact, she was a great fan of sweets - the biggest sweet tooth *I* knew... I don't like them though - "

I was rather surprised. I didn't know a lot of people that weren't too fond of sweets. From my experience it was rare.

"- They give me a stomach-ache. Besides, they are not good for your teeth, and the *worst* thing of all, is to dig out the little pieces that get stuck in your teeth," he finished.

"Oh. Yes, that can be annoying."

"She was a great baker. All kinds of cakes, from cheesecake to -"

"Carrot cake?" I jumped up a little in excitement.

"*Everything* you'd like," he giggled. "I see that someone is waiting for you over there. You should go."

My mother didn't look too happy, but she wasn't angry either, probably because Ela was next to her. She just waved at the man as I walked to her. The flowers that they bought were looking rough and a bit drowsy. Ela, on the other hand, held a marvellous grave lantern. It was small and humble, but I could tell it was well crafted.

"I know Kale, these flowers were the last pair we could get our hands on. We have to make the best of our situation – I would rather buy plastic ones than these, but there weren't any either," my mother said.

The image of the suffering angel popped in my head. It hurt me seeing it in such a state, knowing that it tried its best. "I'm happy with them mum. It's not their fault they're ugly, the seller didn't treat them right."

My mother turned to me for a moment, perplexed to what I've just said. Grandma Ela laughed. I took them from her hand and dropped them in a tall vase that stood proudly on grandpa's stone. We left after we watered them and said a brief prayer. I didn't see the man again.

Back in the car, my mum told me she would pick me up for lunch, when she turned into the side streets.

"And you behave yourself!"

"Yes, mum."

"Do whatever Ela tells you to, is that clear?"

"Yes, mum," I said again, this time rolling my eyes.

"And –"

"Don't be such an ass," Ela interjected.

"Mother! How can you talk to me like that in front of Kale? Watch your language," she swiftly turned into the driveway, braking hard.

"Oh, as if Kale didn't hear that kind of language before. Don't worry, everything will be alright. You should relax more, you're not getting any younger," Ela waddled out of the car giggling. "Come Kale, I got some unfinished pie you have to eat."

When she opened the front door of the house, I got another flash memory. There were so many fond family moments here. From the closest family to the furthest cousins and uncles, this was the house everyone came to visit once in a while. It was strikingly obvious that Ela was the glue of the family, keeping everyone in check, no matter the grudges.

She grabbed a cigarette from the kitchen counter. "Finally! I didn't think I could make it that long, but look at me *haha*!"

I didn't mind her smoking; the whole house was one big smoke sauna anyway. The house itself wasn't too big, but it was enough to have guests and even let them stay over, for a night or two. Her garden was wild, not only was she not interested in keeping it taken care of, but she didn't have a need to do it. According to her, she rarely went out anyway. My mother couldn't stand it. She would do at least a bit of straightening up whenever she came to visit.

"Here you go my dear. What do you want to drink with that?" She held a plate.

"Maybe some tea?"

"Coming right up! Don't hold back, eat as much as you like. I made too much for myself, I can't look at it anymore."

It was a plum pie, with a crispy crust on the outside. When the pies were fresh the plumbs inside were very hot. I have burned myself so often beforehand. I was glad it was cold, because that meant that I could *inhale* that cake like it was nothing.

"Bewishos!" I said with a full mouth.

"What?"

"Delicious! Can I have more?"

"You ate that already? If you want more come and get it yourself. I won't be going back and forth every two seconds."

And so, I did, with lightspeed.

It was just a moment until Ela had no more pie left. She patted me on the shoulder with a proud smile.

"No one can resist the charm of the baking of an elderly woman, *ha*?" She tilted a window open as she held on to a new cigarette.

"Yeah, I guess."

We talked about everything and nothing, about specifics and generalities. About family and strangers. Conversations with Ela were always greatly appreciated. When I said she was the glue of the family, I really meant it. If every family member would have four strings attached to themselves, she would control at least one. It seems off putting when I phrase it like this, but she was the perfect person to have that control. She was harsh, but fair. Funny yet serious. But most importantly – she was loving, behind a thick shell of hardcore stone.

We talked and talked, until she went out for a brief moment to catch her neighbour, who was gardening. Apparently, there were badgers around, disturbing the neighbours' chickens.

In the meantime, I went to the bathroom. I freshened up my hair quickly and left in a rush, but something didn't feel right.

Like in a trance I could hear clattering chains. But there were no chains beside me. Every few moments I could hear a deafening swooshing sound. A slight breeze stroked by my cheeks, and when I blinked, I could see a massive angel stand before me. It was looking right at me. It had lots of chains tied around its neck and wings, but it looked strong enough to bare it.

It bent down to me. "Hmmmm…" It said in such a loud and low voice that I could feel the floor beneath me tremble. "What is your business here?"

I wasn't sure what I was supposed to say. I didn't know the answer to that myself. Intimidated by its grand stature, I stumbled over my words.

"I-I d-don't know."

"Hmmmm…" It said again. "Something has changed in you." It then leaned its massive palms on my shoulders. "Why are you alone?"

"W-What do you mean? Ela invited only *me*, my mum comes to pick me u-"

"Kale… Why is no one guarding you?" It put its left arm behind its back to reach for something. I didn't say anything but shrugged.

"Hmmmm… Take it and spin." It had a massive hourglass in its hands. It was made of rough wood, that splintered all over. The glass was cracked at some places. The sand looked wet and sticky, barely passing through the tiny middle point. When it reached my hands, it transformed gradually. It became smaller and new. The sand was dry again, relieved that it could flow freely.

I gently spun it round, and to my surprise it accelerated faster and faster, until it too was old and broken, like its first state.

"Hmmmm…" It said again, pulling me out of a hypnotising focus. It took the hourglass off me, and when it did, one of its chains grew by another link. "Kasbiele, you are right where you should be. You are not here to learn, but to live, truly. I have seen what was and what will be – where you went, and where you will go."

I couldn't say a word. My fear had shut my mouth closed.

"My dear brother, I wish you farewell in this world."

As it said that it disappeared into smoke, while Ela passed right through.

"Are you alright?" Ela said to me. "You look as if you saw a ghost."

Unbeknownst to her, I did.

For the rest of my stay, I couldn't stop thinking about that angel. I couldn't stop thinking of the coin shores… of Lisa. I knew Ela could tell that something was on my mind, as I zoned out often, no matter what we did, even playing *the* family card game.

"Kale! It's your turn – again." She said. "Is everything alright?"

I just pulled a card from the stack. Ela thought I didn't want to talk, because she became silent as well, only reminding me of my turns from time to time. I felt sorry for her – in my mind I was somewhere else.

She snapped her fingers loudly. "Watch this!" She proceeded to divide her cards into sets in one swift motion and threw the last remaining card onto the discard pile.

I think I gave her a weird look of some kind, because shortly thereafter she came really close and pointed right at me with her finger.

"In cards there is no mercy, even with family."

Ela won the game, like always. She loved to play with me and Marcelina, but she was never a player to go easy on others, no matter how old or how good they were. Poor Ada, she will not have it easy with her. Ela taught every one of us the catchphrase 'During cards there is no coddling'. We all have used it at some point.

"Could I get something to drink?" I asked, laying my defeated cards on the table.

"At last he speaks! I will, only if you promise to continue talking," she pointed at me with her index finger again.

After I nodded, she brought me some orange juice and a bottle of water.

"Are you sure you're alright? I never saw you like this."

Unsure what to tell her I just gulped down all of the juice, trying to come up with something to say. I couldn't just tell her the truth.

"Is it about a girl?" Ela struck out of nowhere. I just looked at her confused, and rather shocked that that was the best she could come up with.

"It is, isn't it?" She slapped the table and laughed. "What is her name you handsome boy? Tell me!"

I hated lying, so I thought I'd use the truth and bend it somewhat.

"Lisa"

"Lisa and Kale, that has a nice ring to it. Do you know her well?" She lit her millionth cigarette.

"I know her very well."

"Oh! Kale, I am so happy! Why didn't you say that in the first place?" She pulled me to her and her accompanying smoke cloud.

I thought of Lisa and how she would react to all of this. I've replayed her death over and over, and it didn't really sink in. Now, though, I understood that I would never see her again.

"When will I meet her, Kale? Or do I know her already?"

"I don't think you will."

Ela's enthusiasm extinguished as fast as it sparked. "Doesn't she like you?"

It reminded me of the feelings I had when I was drowning in the lake. I was lost in there for a finite eternity. I loved her for all her life, and she was taken away from me just like that. A realisation, that I was nothing but a shadow – a convenience. I shed a tear.

"Oh, my dear," she hugged me tighter. "She doesn't deserve you."

Perhaps she didn't.

From then on it wasn't long that my mother came to pick me up. My tears have long been dried up, but my thoughts were still caught in the same web. While my mother waited for me by the car, I tied my shoes by the front door. Ela came to me and said her goodbyes and whispered that my secret would be "kept within these walls". Perhaps it was the sudden rush of fresh air, but as soon as I stepped out the door, I felt exhausted and heavy.

"Hi Kale, how was it?" She asked while she waved at Ela, who still stood by the door.

I didn't respond.

"Seatbelts on?"

"Mhm," I leaned back, nodding off before she set off.

"We're here, Kale."

"W-What?"

"We're home."

Of course, where would I think I would be? The much-needed nap energised me enough to eat and spend a little time with Ada who seemed to be happy to see me. She rustled her annoying little toy that made too much noise, it was her favourite though. Trust me, everyone waited eagerly for her to grow out of it.

The next day began in chaos. Marcelina flew around the house, retrieving things she had left in random places during the weekend. Ada was crying in her crib, while I was shaking it gently, so she could calm down. Mum was shouting at dad, who apparently was in the bathroom too long. She looked at me with surprise:

"Kale! Why aren't you downstairs eating breakfast yet? Don't worry about Ada I will take care of her in a second."

The bathroom door swung open, and my dad ran out shirtless to the living room. "The shirt is on the couch, it's all washed and ironed."

"Thank you my dear!" Dad said rushing down the stairs.

When I got there too, I prepared my favourite cereal. Much like my favourite spread, it was chocolate flavoured.

"First!" Said Marcelina to me, jumping from her seat of the dinner table, taking her empty plate to the kitchen. I just started to pour the milk in the bowl.

The real pressure was the moment I could hear dad turn on the car on the driveway. I don't know what it was, but I chugged down the milk with the cereal, almost choking. It was like an instinct, but I was afraid of something at that moment. Mum stood by the door with Ada in her hands waiting for me.

"Have fun in school," she told me while I waddled out with my heavy backpack in my hands.

The drive to school always lasted long, as we lived in the suburbs. The car ride was always a relaxing one, because I didn't have to do anything, just wait. Marcelina was on her phone the whole time, my dad was focused on the road ahead, so I just stared out the window.

As soon as we entered the school, I saw my sister leave me entirely. Weirdly enough that was the last time I saw her until the ride back home. The hallways were large and people all around were chatting, rushing, and unpacking, including the teachers.

"Hey," I heard someone shout across to me. "Hold up!" It was a rather frail boy wearing a T-shirt with cartoon characters on it.

"How was your weekend?" he asked panting from the run to me.

"It was all good Andrew. We went to church yesterday, I liked it a lot."

"Church? I overslept for that. We had a football match on Saturday. We won, but now my legs are giving up on me." His laugh was so specific, it could sparked memories.

"Are you alright, Kale?" Andrew continued.

"W-Why do you ask?"

"For starters you went to church yesterday. That is a big change ain't it? Plus, you don't seem right."

"I'm just a bit dizzy, but thanks for asking." My head was aching quite a bit, but I was sure that it would stop eventually. He then overtook me just before the entrance to class 412.

The room was surrounded by colourful posters on the walls, stickers on large windows and big shelves with objects, toys, and geometric shapes. The teacher wasn't there yet so everyone fooled around.

Scanning the room, I knew who was there at an instant. A shy girl in the back of the room, that fiddled with braids, that was Margot. The noisy group in the centre, that was impossible to miss, was made up of David, George, Sandra, Peter, and Andrew. On the left though, sitting just next to a poster saying, "OuR fAvOuRiTe DiNoSaUrS", was Caroline. Every time I looked at her, I had a strange feeling, it was an uneasy feeling in my stomach, but despite that I felt light and energized. I was set on high alert. Even though I wanted to go to her, I avoided her, and went to my seat on the second-last row.

"Kale! What's up?" David jumped at me. "I finally beat the boss on *Parla de Taux*! You were right, once you use all your mana potions your increased energy levels directly increase your damage output. I usually like to save all my potions for future enemies... at least I finally passed that level."

To fill you in, Parla de Taux was a video game where you played the fictional character Parla in an exotic adventure setting, trying to find unique objects, such as talismans, trophies, emeralds and so forth. On the way you were bound to meet enemies of different types. I loved that game, but I finished it already – I wasn't a fan of re-playing video games I've completed.

"Ah! Good to know. Have you found the key in the cavern?"

"What key - what cavern?" His eyes popped open. "What cavern? What cavern!?"

I laughed at his sense of urgency. "Just after beating the boss, besides the obvious front opening, there is a smaller crack to the right side. When you go through it there is a cavern with lots of gold and diamonds, but most importantly there is a key that you will be able to use for - "

"Okay! Don't tell me everything! Thanks for the tip." As quickly as he came to me, he left to his group to continue their funny pranks.

Just as I opened my notebook, Mrs Harding greeted the class in a high-pitched voice. Everyone settled down and took their seats. From there the lesson began. The subject was English if you were curious. We spent most of the time talking about a book that I didn't like at all. At least I read it, not like many of my classmates. Anyhow, the last subject of the school day was Geography, where we had the test.

The nervousness was in the air. Those who studied a lot were scared not to do well, and those who didn't study at all, rather weirdly, were the beacons of positivity. They had no care in the world which probably served them well. But me? I was scared. It was interesting how a simple piece of paper could produce so much anxiety and pressure. I never got used to that.

After the test school finally ended. Ben caught me on my way out.

"Kale! Thanks for helping to study for the test. It really helped me. Me and a couple friends of mine will be playing football in the park this Friday after school. Would be awesome if you could join! I miss hanging out with you *man*."

"I will tell you tomorrow, is that alright?"

"Sure thing!"

I waved at him while hopping into the backseat. My sister was already waiting, mocking me for my sluggishness. It was tiring, all the talking, walking around, studying. Oh, and don't get me started with the clock that seemed to know how to slow down during the most awkward and difficult moments in class.

"How was school Marcelina?" Dad asked, waiting at a traffic light.

"Fine."

"When is it ever not?" I saw dad become a little irritated in the mirror. To make him feel a bit better I forced myself to speak, even though I really didn't want to.

"I had a good day, dad."

"Is that so?" His eyes sparkled slightly.

"Yeah… I think I did well on the geography test we had today. It was about rivers."

"Ah, that is good to hear. Back when *I* was at school Geography was my least favourite subject, I will have you know," he giggled. "Remembering all countries, and their cities, rivers. Looking at hills and fields and rocks and…". I stopped listening at that point. Of course, I nodded and occasionally responded, but my mind wandered elsewhere. It was not the first time a simple conversation led my parents to lead an endless monologue about their life.

It took me till Thursday to finally convince my parents (mostly mom) to go out play football. When that day came, I rocked up to school looking like a pack donkey. I could barely walk up the stairs with the bags I had to carry. School that day took ages to finish. Honestly; I didn't learn anything that day. All my thoughts were stolen by my excitement.

When the final bell rang, me, Ben, and other friends grouped up and walked across the street to the park. There was an open field of grass where we could play deep inside the park, past a dense ring of trees. With the weight of the bags it felt like I was hurdling over the roots, and surely enough I happened to trip over one. Behind the immediate pain of dirt and small pebbles crashing into my face I heard a burst of laughter.

"Oh crap!" One of them shouted.

"Kale, are you ok?" Ben said, coming up to me. "That was a hard hit." He then took my bags aside and lifted me up.

"I'm fine Ben, thanks." I was so embarrassed. I brushed off my face and arms. After a quick inspection, the bags took the worst of it, but after a simple sweep there was nothing to show for the fall except for my red face.

We then arrived at the 'pitch' and played in the park. It was a blast! I think there were around 15 of us. I wasn't the best, but I didn't care. I just loved to be around my friends outside school for a change.

Long into the game there was a moment where the ball was chased by Ben and Henrik, one of Ben's friends outside of school. Despite the agreed rule of no sliding, Ben tackled Henrik aggressively. Henrik was furious. Arms were swinging all over the place and some of us quickly huddled the players. From one moment to the next, it became dead quiet. When I approached them, I could see why. Ben was lying on the ground, motionless. His face was swelling up rather quickly.

"Get back Henrik!" I heard one of us say. "Get back!"

He did take a couple steps back. He was panting in anger. There was no mistaking it was serious, as he stood there with clenched fists. It was odd, as if someone took control over him, because there was a moment where he regained his composure.

And as soon as he did, he took off, leaving behind everything and everyone.

It was a mess. Nobody knew what to do and many froze as motionless as Ben. I took it upon myself to help Ben out.

"Do you know what to do?" I cried out to the group. "Anyone?"

Nobody answered. I didn't know what to do either. In this loneliness I envisioned quickly reappearing images of a woman lying on a kitchen floor, but I didn't know why, or who it was.

"Where are you taking him?" One of the boys behind me asked.

I found myself carrying him in my arms. The weight became overwhelming all of a sudden, but I was close to the road. I was breathing heavily, grunting during every step. A woman, possibly a mother, rushed to me.

"What is wrong?"

In the attempt of laying him down, he slipped out of my hands, and I dropped him halfway down onto the pavement.

"Tell me what happened," she said impatiently.

"I'm not really sure." I really wasn't. I saw what happened from afar, and the most of it was covered by the group that gathered around it.

The woman didn't think twice about calling the ambulance. I just stood there obeying her every command, because it seemed to me that she knew what she was doing. Plus, I gathered it was rude not to listen to someone older. The wait for the ambulance was longer than I expected, and for the entire time Ben remained unconscious.

"Don't worry, everything will be okay," she said as soon as she found time for me. I couldn't respond. Everything went so fast, I tried to keep up. Like a curse, all that came out of my mouth was another grunt.

"Hey! What's your name?"

"Ehm, K-Kale"

"Everything will be fine Kale, do you understand? Your friend is just asleep right now." She was aggressively snapping her fingers at me. "Kale. Kale! Don't look at him anymore. Look at me."

I couldn't see any rush or worry from her when she cared for Ben. She for sure liked brown, because everything she wore was in a shade of brown, except for her hat. It was a sun hat... a red sun hat, with imprints of bright flowers all around it. Like fields of rapeseed on a sunny day, it was impossible to take your eyes off. Stretching endlessly, meeting clouds on the tip of a hill, one could stand and wonder what would be on the other side. More fields? Perhaps a forest? What about a mighty castle that once was showered by fame, but now was kept secret by the lone farmer of the fields? When you think about it, wouldn't he become the guardian of the castle? Once he leaves or dies the next farmer would replace him. Over the years there would be a line of unrelated farmers staying true to their oath of the castle. But what would the castle be called? What about 'Junior castle'... No, that sounds too modern. 'Pulululu castle'? No that is just plain stupid. What about...

"Kale!" the woman dragged me away from Ben, who was still lying on the pavement.

Two men in bright visibility jackets kneeled next to Ben, opening a big bag. "Hello? Can you hear me?" One of them asked, slapping Ben lightly on the face. "Hel-"

"Come here Kale." The woman pulled me around and hugged me. "You are so brave... so, so brave."

It was a few days later that I went to the hospital to see Ben. Mum was there with me. The room was difficult to find, but after some walking, we finally got there.

"Room 328, here we go." Mum smiled at me.

Just then a nurse came out of the room. Surprised to see us, she said, "Oh, Mrs Ingram I'm guessing."

"Yes, thank you for letting us see Ben. It does mean a lot, especially to Kale here."

"I'm sure it does," the nurse smiled at me. "Can I talk to you for a moment?" She said to my mum.

While they talked, I stood there in front of the door. I couldn't help it, but my hands were shaking. A thousand thoughts flooded me at once, but before I could decipher any of them, mum came back.

"Kale… I'm sorry, but Ben doesn't feel well right now."

"Can we still see him?"

"I'm afraid not. We need to come another time."

The curse continued from there. "Don't worry Kale, next time we will see him for sure!"

Surprisingly, I wasn't disappointed. It was as if I knew that it wouldn't work out all along. I would be surprised if we *did* get in. Nonetheless, I saw that my mum was worried. The drive home was erratic and impatient, but we didn't rush anywhere. It was also one of the rare rides where we didn't talk in the car. I tried to occupy myself by being on my phone. When I opened it, I saw that David wrote me a message.

'Hey! Did you hear about that? I can't wait. Please wait up for me, I didn't finish the first part yet.'

After that, I saw that David sent me a link to a website. My eyes popped and I cried out in victory. Mum suddenly applied the brake for a moment.

"Kale! Don't scare me like that! Why did you do that?"

"There is a sequel!"

"A sequel? To what?"

"Parla de Taux."

"Oh, that's great! I would appreciate it if you wouldn't scare me like that while I'm driving. It's not the safest thing to do... you know, I'm driving."

After a quick apology I texted David till we were home. And when we got home, I rushed to the computer to do more research. It turned out that the new game, *Parla de Taux: The beginnings*, would be set before the original game, where Parla embarked onto his first adventures. I had no clue how that evaded me, because I was looking forward to it since the developers announced its release last year.

For a short time the new video game was all I could think and talk about. Everything else wasn't important. However, much to my misery, I forced myself to hold on to getting the game, so I could play together with David. Because of that, school was only useful to see his progress in the original game. It took him three weeks to finish it. Three weeks! I was so proud that I held on for so long.

Chapter Three

The way to school was all ordinary, in fact the whole week was. A cycle of school, homework, and sleep trapped me. In this routine all highlights blended into its greyness. For a moment to become special, something big must happen. And so, the time came.

The morning was as ordinary as it gets. I ate the same chocolate cereal as any other day. The ride to school was experienced in a half-dead, tired haze. When I entered my classroom, the same, old posters greeted me, but what stood out like a sore thumb, was a boy smiling directly at me.

"Ben! I-I can't believe it! What are you doing here?"

"Hi Kale, awesome to see you too!" He laughed.

Stunned by the surprise, I didn't know what to say next. I had so many questions. I dropped my bag and came to him for a hug.

"Don't squeeze too hard," his voice trembled a bit.

"Fine... It's just such a nice surprise. How are you, Ben? I came to visit you, a week ago, but we couldn't enter."

"I know. I appreciate it Kale, I really do. It took me a while to get better. I'm still not perfect, but good enough I guess."

I saw he didn't want to talk about it anymore. His face looked much better than what it was in the park. Not wanting to make him feel bad during his very first day back in school I went back to my seat to get ready for the lesson.

During the day I saw many students and teachers shower him with questions. I made sure to ignore him because of that, so I didn't become another weight he needed to pull.

That day, mum, together with Ela, picked me up from school.

"What is she wearing? Are you seeing this? Her jeans have such big holes in them that I thought she was caught by a combine." I heard Ela say the moment I opened the door. "Hey sucker, how you doin'?"

"I'm great! School was exciting for once!" I said.

"Well, that's a change, good to hear honey," mum said.

"Why are you here?" I asked Ela.

"Didn't want to see you either," Ela winked at me in the mirror. "I just thought I'd come for a visit."

"We have some stuff to plan, some boring things that adults do, you know?" Mum added.

"Alright, but will we play cards?" I asked.

"We will see," mum started the car and reversed from the parking space.

"We will see? What the hell, of course we will. I can't believe my ears," Ela scoffed.

I smiled.

I finished my homework and scurried downstairs to the living room. As soon as she saw me, mum stood up and said loudly, "Oh Kale, already done?"

I could see dad, Ela, and my uncle pause their conversation.

"Oh, hi Uncle Tom," I went to him.

"Hello there, Kale."

"I didn't know you'd be here," I said.

"I'm sorry, I didn't fill you in," mum came to me. "We have something important to discuss. Could you go upstairs and play?"

"But Ela said we could play cards today," I answered.

"Well, we haven't finished yet, I will come get you as soon as we are done here, okay?"

I nodded and went back up. I was on my phone until my mum opened the door.

"We are ready. Come down, I made a little something to eat."

I saved my progress, and headed down immediately. At the front door I saw Uncle Tom.

"You're already leaving? I thought you'd play too," I said to him.

"I have to go home I'm afraid. We will play next time, I promise," he offered his pinkie finger.

I accepted his offer.

"Bye now," he said. "Enjoy your meal."

"Thank you"

Mum baked a cake. It was a chocolate cake with a thick cream in the middle. A family classic, made quickly and easily from a packet, but it was delicious.

"Take a piece or two and let's go," Ela said from the backdoor. She was smoking, puffing everything out of the opened door.

Mum was already sitting at the table shuffling the cards. We began playing shortly after.

"You said that you had a great school day, right?" Mum asked, dealing the cards.

"Yes, Ben came back."

"Is that the one who got a bit of a knock?" Ela licked her fingers slightly in order to help her fan out the cards.

"That isn't funny," mum said. "He got hurt."

"His face still looks rough, but much better than it was," I said.

"It must've been weird to go back to school after that," mum said.

"Yeah, it would be," Ela threw out a card to the discard pile. "Kale, if you get into a *situation*, I want to see that the other person looks worse than you. Do you understand?"

"Ela is just joking, don't listen to her," mum said.

"No, I'm not. Stop taking things I say and water them down. I am old enough to have the right to say what I think. I said what I said and you better deal with it," Ela smacked down another card. "Kale, when someone attacks you first, you have the right to beat the living crap out of them. Do you hear me?"

I looked at mum, but she stayed silent, turning a bit red.

"I'm not saying you go around punching everyone you see. If I ever hear about a *situation* where you attacked someone without a reason, I will come to you and do the same to you. I know where you live," Ela pointed with her finger again. "I may be old, but don't test me."

I couldn't say a word, and just tried to play the game. My heart was racing, and I had to press my teeth together to hold my fear in.

Of course, Ela won the first couple rounds.

After a seemingly long time of silence mum said, "When it comes to Ben, wouldn't you want to invite him over? After such a horrible thing, I think it would be nice for you to reconnect."

"Do you mean it?" I felt my eyes stretch out. "That would be so awesome!"

"Of course, I think it would be a great idea," mum said. "Just go and ask when they have time, and we can arrange it."

"Can David come too?" I said.

"I wouldn't see why not, one guest, or two. There is not a big difference," mum answered.

"You're lucky your mum is soft," Ela obviously joked, holding in a laugh. "My parents would only allow me to have friends over if they would help out with chores. Back then you had to deserve it."

"Really, like washing dishes, or doing the ironing?" I was interested.

"No, like feeding the chickens in the pen, sweeping the drive or front porch, mowing the lawn…"

"Oh no, that doesn't sound like fun. I hate mowing the lawn," I said.

"I know," Grandma Ela winked.

Suddenly, Ela coughed. She had the smoker's cough, which was full of rasp and you could hear that it came from the deep. But that time she couldn't stop.

She turned away, not to cough onto the table, and spread her arms next to her lowered head. Mum, with an open palm, smacked her hard on the back a couple times.

"Thank you," Ela regained her composure.

"That is why you never touch cigarettes Kale," mum said.

"No, no. The cigarettes are not the problem. The real problem is when you don't have a child of your own to hit you when you need it," Ela laughed. "These were some proper hits you know."

Ela seemed proud of mum, but mum rolled her eyes and went on to win the round of cards.

"My problem is your lack of skill," mum said.

I laughed, and Ela stood up to go for a smoke.

"During cards, there is no coddling," I said.

The game lasted till the evening. No big surprise that I lost, but I was proud that I was getting better. The next day I asked Ben and David about whether they would want to come to ours. We arranged a day for a sleepover at our house. It was during the weekend of course, so we had loads of time and we would potentially stay up all night.

When the day had finally come, I cleaned like my life depended on it. Everything my mum asked of me was a command that I fulfilled with a smile from ear to ear. I helped do the dishes, vacuum the living room, dust off the entrance, reorganised the shoe rack, ordered my books back into alphabetical order... I did the lot. It was all worth it, because once the doorbell rang, there was no stopping. I was jumping at the door, waiting for my mum to come and welcome them home. I didn't do it because I was too shy in front of Ben's parents.

"Welcome! Just open the gate with a bit of force – there you go," mum said.

"Thank you! Kids you go do your thing." Once the order was given, Ben and David ran up to the porch and stormed the entry.

"Hello Mrs. Ingram."

"Hi, guys! How are we today?"

"We are great! Thank you for letting us sleep over, we are so excited!" Said Ben.

David made sure not to be rude and finished the formalities, "Yes ma'am, thank you so much!"

"I can see that you three are buzzing out of excitement," mum said.

"Before you storm off, take your things with you!" Ben's mum said at the porch already, holding two large bags. Ben and David snatched them, and we ran upstairs to my room.

"Thank you for inviting us over," I could hear Ben's mum say behind the loud thumping noise of the stairs.

"It's a pleasure! Tea or coffee – "

"*Man*, we will play all night!" David drooled over his imagination.

"First let's get to my room and unpack, then we can begin."

They threw the bags onto my bed, ruining my neatly positioned blankets and pillows. They both looked around in confusion.

"Weren't your walls white before?" both asked.

Yes, they were. I forgot about it already, because it was some time ago since me and dad painted the not-so-white walls into a very-blue colour.

"Oh, yeah. No *biggie*. You like it?"

Both of them nodded, whilst unpacking their stuff. There were three days' worth of clothes inside their bags. My parents would do that too. 'Spare T-shirt just in case. Better yet, have a spare for your spare', I could imagine them saying.

Once they unpacked, we headed to the small guest room next door. It had the console and TV there, as my parents weren't very keen on the idea of me having my own TV. Probably a good idea, as I wouldn't get a lot of work done.

Mum and I placed a mattress in front of the TV so we can all sit together and play. We planted the snacks to either side and started playing hours on end. Many moments were mind boggling in the story plot. The levels were much more difficult than we had expected, and the new graphics just sucked us in completely.

"Dinner is ready!" mum barged in. "Oh gosh, those sheets will never be clean again," she laughed. We had crumbs lying everywhere, never mind the controller – it was filthy and all slippery, but we didn't care.

"Alright mom! We'll be down just after we finish this level, it's nearly the end."

"Ok, see you there! We will start without you."

The level we were trying to beat entailed travelling to a town. Seemed easy, but we were stuck on it. It looked like this:

We were in a tundra, far away from any checkpoints. Our objective was to cross a large valley, from one hillside to the other. The tricky part was that in the valley there was a flowing river, which was so cold, it couldn't be crossed safely. Everything was covered in leafless bushes, dying trees and hard soil or gravel, masked with a thin sheet of hardened snow, or ice. Whenever we began the mission, we had to tread carefully, as in the bushes poisonous insects lingered. If we were too careful, at some point we would be tracked down by either large lynxes or wolves.

We were stuck on this level for so long, that we gave up and chose another adventure in the menu later on.

We went down to smell the amazing food! Mum made homecooked lasagne and cookies for dessert. I knew that the following days would be extra healthy, so I crammed it in like there was no tomorrow. Not only did I, but all three of us looked like starved pigs with smothered cheeks. Under the light I could see fat stains on David's glasses. Marcelina couldn't take a lot of our smacking and slurping, so she went to her room to eat there. Her loss, more for us!

We went back to our boy-cave with filled stomachs.

"Hey, Kale, tell me something. I've noticed you rarely talk to Caroline. During the project where you were together with her and me, you seemed so different. You talked only when spoken to, and you didn't look at me or her even once." David said.

"Sounds like you like her!" Ben said.

"No, come on, it's not like that," I panicked. "She isn't my type at all."

"Yeah right," Ben opened yet another pack of sweets. "*Man*, just tell us *man*, we won't do anything."

"Well – it might be that she is a bit – interesting."

"Oh! It's true!" They both jumped up in excitement.

"Don't tell anyone, please!" I was worried.

"Why don't you go and tell her? Just go *man*," Ben munched on a piece of chocolate.

"I don't know how."

"Mrs Harding told us that we would go outside to learn about different types of trees, and afterwards we will play in the park. If that is not a *perfect* place then I don't know what is," David said.

"You sure?" I remained highly sceptical.

"You can trust us, *man*. What's the worst that can happen?"

The time at the park was really fun. We looked at oak trees, chestnut, birch, and apple. There was one in particular that was really beautiful. It was a cherry tree. After having looked at them and analysed their leaves, we had to write a little summary, sketching the leaves the best we could. I didn't do too well; I wasn't a good drawer.

With that done, we were free to go to the playground at the park close by. There were slides, swings, wooden forts, and all sorts of ropes. Ben came to me when I was already a sweaty mess.

"Did you do it yet?" He said.

"No. I don't think this is a good idea," I tried to convince him.

"I don't want to be that guy, but if you don't do it, I will tell her myself."

"No! Please, no."

"Then do it. Come on *man*, don't be a chicken," Ben said. "Good luck".

The panic started to kick in. Just the thought of what he asked me to do made me sick. When I searched for her, I found her sitting on the bench by herself. Everything inside me fluttered and sung, but the sick feeling took over quickly again. My forehead started sweating, my stomach growled in disagreement. Even my voice didn't want to sound anymore. But I forced myself to go to her. It just took a moment until I reached her, but from my perspective it lasted hours. Hours of deliberating and debating this idea – planning a way out of this somehow.

When I reached her, I completely forgot what I wanted to say. I just stood in front of her, staring.

"Kale, you're creeping me out," she said looking at me with some kind of disgust.

"Oh, sorry, I didn't want to do that." I played with my fingers in distress. "Can I talk to you?"

I made the mistake of not listening to her answer, and just sat down. She was either appalled or confused, I couldn't tell. Not the best of starts, but I was too deep into this. I couldn't just bail.

She waited patiently. Her eyes really got me weak. I never talked to her before, so I panicked. I didn't know what to say to make it better, so I just said it directly, "S-So, Caroline. I like you."

The world stood still, and I felt my inner voice clapping sarcastically in a slow pace. My tongue paralysed itself and my brain just threw itself into a shredder.

"What?" Caroline laughed. "You came here to tell me that you like me?"

All I could do was nod.

I could tell she didn't know what to do with that information. She just prolonged the laugh, stood up and left.

The fluttering stopped. So did the sweating and twitching. My mind just went dark as my fear had come true. I wished I could just disappear into the wind, or just blend in with the bench – in my mind I did. I couldn't stand up, no matter how much I wanted to leave. My friends played in laughter, zooming from one side of the playground to the other. The hard bench remained my only companion, until somebody sat down next to me.

"Kale? Is everything alright?" I looked up to see Mrs Harding wearing a straw sun hat and holding a sandwich in her hand. "What happened?"

"I just don't feel like playing, Mrs Harding," I kept on fumbling my fingers.

"Why is that? I saw you having fun in there," she pointed at the big wooden house in the centre.

"Yeah, I did, I just don't feel like it anymore."

"Alright, can I stay here with you? The sandwich is amazing!" She smiled and handed me the other half from a wrapper. "It's with ham and cheese, if you'd like."

It's not the first time she shared things with us. She brought self-made cookies whenever the class averaged a test higher than 80%. I knew I was hungry, but I really didn't feel like eating, so I declined the offer.

We sat in silence for the rest of the time our class was outside. My emotions were all over the place. On one hand I wanted to be left alone, but on the other I felt comfort not sitting all by myself. I didn't really know what I wanted, or what to do.

When we lined up in pairs to go back to school. I didn't talk to anyone and Ben insisted I told him what happened – but I couldn't hear him. I just watched the dirt and stones pass by as we walked along the park path. It went on like this for the rest of the day, until my dad asked me why I was staring at my dinner.

"Seems like you didn't have the best of days buddy," he chuckled, trying to cheer me up with a rub on the shoulder. "During days like these, son, you just have to survive. It will be better, no doubt. Right Marcelina?"

She didn't say anything, but I could sense she nodded. I guessed she wasn't that interested anyway, lucky me.

"Eat at your own pace honey. You don't have to eat now. I can always heat it up for you later."

We did that quite often. Whenever someone didn't have the appetite for some reason or another, the plate was either put in the fridge or, if untouched, poured back into the pans that were on the stove. For us it wasn't important *when* you eat, but *that* you eat. Throwing away prepared food was a big no-no. I once had to eat a piece of meat that I had laid off for three days, because it was already hard then. Unsurprisingly, it didn't get much softer. It felt like a boulder passing through my throat.

I skipped dinner then, walking up those endless stupid stairs that sucked the life out of me, not only in school, but also at home. The silence the moment I pushed my door shut, was bliss.

The next school day began like any other. But still ashamed from what had happened, I didn't look forward to talking in school. Ben, though, didn't deserve my silence.

"What happened *man*?" He asked. "I know it's bad, obviously. But what exactly did she say?"

"She laughed," I said.

"And nothing else?"

I answered with silence.

"That is bad. I'm sorry to hear that. Word is going around about you liking her. We all know. I saw Caroline talk to the other girls. I'm happy you tried, that takes bravery."

I didn't think that way, but sure. School till summer won't be fun, that's for sure.

And it wasn't, it was brutal. I didn't realise it, but when I asked her, I had put all my cards on the table. There were no secrets left that they would hunt me for. Walking around the hallways felt like public shaming, and there was nothing I could do about it. I didn't look at Caroline for the rest of the school year – luckily we had only two months left till summer break. Every passing week was another week survived.

One fateful night, before school, I had a nightmare. Such a horrible one in fact, that I jumped up in the darkness, sweating and breathing heavily. I couldn't hear the grasshoppers chirp, nor the wind. Everything was like in a painting. I flipped the whole duvet off me, feeling my sweat strike the cool air. The small droplets glistened in the full moon. I was afraid. Not of the nightmare, because I escaped that already, but of something else. When my breath stabilised, I sat up, with my feet dangling off the edge of my bed and my palms resting against the soft mattress. I looked at my poster-filled walls and found comfort in them.

"Man up," I said to myself. "It's been weeks, probably everyone forgot about that already."

'You are absolutely right,' I imagined the poster saying. 'There is nothing to be afraid of.'

It really helped me calm down and go back to sleep. It was during breakfast when I had forgotten all about my nightmare. At school, during the lunch break, Marcelina came to me.

"We will get a taxi home," she said.

"Why?" I was confused.

"Mum and dad have something to figure out. Not sure exactly. After school ends, meet me here, okay? I will phone one for us."

And it happened just as she said. She paid the driver with her pocket money. When we stood at the front porch of our house, Marcelina turned one of the vases sideways, to reveal a key.

"Never thought I'd use that," she mumbled to herself and opened the door.

"Who's there?" we could hear the nanny from upstairs.

"Kale and Marcelina," I shouted up.

Usually when things got busy, we got a nanny for Ada. It was always the same guy. He studied and did this as an extra job, my mum told me once. I liked him, but he took the job too seriously, so I could never do anything with him.

We took off our shoes and went to the living room, sitting on the couch. I turned on the TV and got lost in it, trying to suppress my hunger. Marcelina tapped away on her phone.

"Your parents told me to leave as soon as you came," the guy came to us. "Ada is alright, we played for the whole time, now she is tired and went for a nap."

"Thank you," Marcelina said.

"See you around," he said, putting his shoes on and leaving.

Two episodes later I turned down the volume, because we could hear a car drive into our driveway.

"Stay there," Marcelina said. She peaked out of the window. "Yeah, it's mum and dad."

We waited for the sound of slamming doors, but it didn't come.

"I'll go check if everything is okay. Do you want to come too?" She asked me.

"No, you go ahead," I put the volume back up.

With every minute that she was gone I grew more impatient and worried. I stood up and peeked out the window myself.

I saw all three of them there, but nothing seemed wrong, so I went upstairs. I changed into my comfy trousers, throwing the jeans onto my bed. I put on a looser T-shirt too. Then suddenly Marcelina slammed the door open in an outburst of anguish. She flew into my arms, hugging me tightly. I felt her tears go through my upper sleave. I wasn't sure what had happened, but it for sure was nothing good.

"Kale! Ela passed away this morning."

I immediately felt sick. Goosebumps rushed through me. My mouth twitched.

"W-What?"

She didn't respond, and for a while we just stayed motionless and in silence.

"No, this can't be. We saw her just a few days ago!" I said.

All the memories together played back in my head. All the family meetings in her house. The card games, the cakes and pies, the laughter. It all suddenly felt so grey now. I heard mum and dad come in through the main door. Mum's cry echoed in the house.

"This can't be," I said out loud. "It can't be."

"It's true," Marcelina said.

I had to stay strong, for my sister. I had to stay calm. My lips couldn't move properly, so I decided to not talk. To help her, I thought, I had to *do* something.

"Do you want some hot chocolate?" I shared my idea.

"Mhm," her grip loosened.

"I will go down and get it for you, I will be right back."

When I reached the final steps of the stairs, I saw mum curled up on her knees, still in her shoes. Dad was consoling her. My dad looked over to me. His eyes gave out peace and understanding, but it was obvious he too was broken. I went on to the kitchen and decided to make hot chocolate for everyone. One spoon of cocoa for Marcelina, two for my parents, and four for myself. Having put the drinks for my parents on the table, I took mine and Marcelina's upstairs. I then noticed how calm my hands were. Usually, I'd spill some of it, but not this time.

"Here you go," I said to Marcelina, who laid on her bed buried in duvets and pillows. Through it, I could hear a muffled "Thank you."

I thought it would be best to leave her alone for now, so I went to check on Ada. I cracked open the door slightly, which was a difficult task due to its loud nature. I peeked to see her stand on her bed, leaning onto the banister without giving out a single peep. When I opened the door fully and came in, I startled her, and she fell on her backside – still without anything to say.

Ada had it nice. Not understanding what it meant for someone to leave. She wouldn't remember all of that anyway. She stared at me smiling and rocking her toy in front of me vigorously.

"Sure, I'll play," I said to her.

It felt as if I knew this would happen all along. It didn't take long until, with Ada's help, I forgot about what had happened.

I saw Ada reaching for my nearly emptied glass, which cooled down by this point. "Do you want it?" I pointed at it. Ada tried to say words, but just high-pitched noises came out. "Sure, you want it! Take the straw in your hand" I leaned the glass towards her, holding it tightly.

Ada grabbed the straw with both hands and sucked as hard as she could. But when she wanted to breath out, she breathed through the straw as well, so violently in fact that the remainder exploded onto me and her.

My white T-shirt wasn't that pristine anymore, but Ada didn't help. She yelled in laughter and smeared more of it around my chest. As the T-shirt was ruined anyway, we might as well have some fun with it. I smeared some of the warm chocolate on her face. I burst out laughing too, when she rotated her tongue around her mouth as far as she could, trying to lick everything.

When the chaos dried up, dad came in.

"Nice to see you two," he said. "Just checking in. Marcelina doesn't feel too good."

His red and baggy eyes reminded me of what just happened.

"Sorry for the mess, we just wanted to play," I said.

"I understand. Thank you for the chocolate, it's very sweet of you."

Ada reached out for dad, mumbling some gibberish. Dad picked her up and rocked her up and down, side to side.

"Kale, you seem fine, but I know it must be hard. Do you want to talk about it?"

I wasn't sure. I felt guilty that I wasn't as sad as everybody else. Did that mean I didn't like her as much as everybody else? But it was Ela! I liked her so much!

"It's fine if you don't want to. We can talk any time you want. I will go back to mum. Can you continue looking after Ada? You're doing a great job."

I nodded.

That day dinner was self-service. No TV's blared across the rooms, no typing could be heard. No strict bedtime too.

Not a single tear was of my making that day.

I woke up because of the roar of morning traffic. I wondered why nobody woke me up for school. I brushed my teeth quickly and put on the first clothes I saw in my cupboard. I threw my notebooks into my bag and ran down. But nobody was there.

"Mum? Dad?" I looked around.

The kitchen was empty, the living room too. I checked the driveway and dad's car was missing.

"We are not going to school."

I flinched.

Marcelina appeared out of nowhere.

"Why?" I said.

"Why? Guess," she said facepalming her forehead. She then quickly changed her demeanour. "Sorry Kale, I didn't mean it."

"It's okay. So, what do we do?" I sat down at the table.

"Whatever you want, whatever you need to do," Marcelina took out an ice-cream from the freezer. "Do you want some?"

"For breakfast?"

She nodded while piercing the new bucket of ice cream with a spoon.

"Yeah."

She handed me some and went back up, stopping in the middle of the stairs.

"I will watch a movie. Do you want to join?" she said.

I ran up, leaving my bag downstairs.

"Is mum okay?" I asked, making myself comfortable on her bed, leaning my head against the wall cushioned by a pillow.

"I mean, as good as you can expect," she unplugged her laptop and sat next to me. "You went to sleep early, we were checking up on you, but you kept sleeping. We didn't want to wake you."

"What did you guys do?" I started eating my ice cream.

"We talked, like for a long time. It was horrible. Not the talk, but the atmosphere obviously. I don't want to talk about it too much. Mum will tell you everything they told me today. Just let her sleep for now."

The movie began.

This was the norm for the next two to three days. Lots of movies were watched, and many hours were spent alone with one's thoughts. Mum and dad often left the house to prepare everything. During the weekend my cousins came from overseas to stay at ours. Mum's endless phone calls, as well as dad's, revealed more family was arriving all around town.

Just like that on Tuesday morning, I was sitting in the car with mum and Marcelina on the way to the funeral.

"Dad is already there. We had to organise some things".

"It's okay mum," Marcelina said beside me.

"How are you holding up you two? If it's going to be too much, just tell me and you can leave the ceremony. No one would blame you," mum looked at me through the mirror.

"I think we're both alright, right?" I said.

"Mhm"

When we pulled up next to the church, everyone was there already, dressed in black and all of them were either looking at the ground, or hugging someone else. There were many more people I didn't know than I expected.

"Go inside, first row to the right. Dad is waiting for you," mum told us, before setting off into a different direction.

At the entrance there was a poster on the wall that had a picture of Ela and her name. I felt offended by it. She was so much more than just a picture. The thought that I would end up as a picture and a name too made me want to rip it all apart.

In the church, whispers echoed and so did the heels of elderly women. A casket at the altar showered with flowers stood menacingly enough to make me uneasy. And yet it reflected the candle lights, leaving a beautiful black and glossy surface.

"Don't look there, Kale, it will only make you sadder," dad said.

"Hmm?"

"The casket. It isn't a pleasant sight. We will sit together, but you have the choice to sit here in the first row, or in the second. It's your choice."

"Second!" Marcelina cried out, and without hesitation squeezed herself onto the bench, reaching into her pocket.

"Alright, but no phone. Give it to me."

"What? No wai-"

"There's no discussion."

Marcelina surrendered, sitting and watching what was unfolding around her.

"And you Kale?"

I thought about it. I felt that this was my chance to say goodbye to Ela, and I didn't want to do it hiding in the back row. "Ela would be happy to see me in the first row, even though I'm not too keen."

"Choosing where to sit will show nothing significant. It's only for you to feel more comfortable. Trust me, Ela is happy to see you brave enough to be here, saying goodbye," dad hugged me. "If you sit in the front row, I will be sitting next to you, big guy."

Dad's sincerity had the ability to calm you down when moments were tough. This was no exception. It seemed he always knew what the right thing was to say.

Not long after, the extended family came to us also in suits and dresses. At least there was one thing good about funerals, among all the bad – it was a reason for the whole family to come together. I hadn't seen my cousins for a couple years now. The last time, rather unfortunately, was the funeral of a distant uncle I didn't know much about. Just about when mum joined us, we all scrambled to our seats. There were still whispers all around, but they immediately died down, when the organs started playing.

The 'official' church proceedings went by quickly.

"Everyone is here to say goodbye to dear Elisabeth. For some she was a work colleague, for some a friend. The lucky ones among you can count her as family. I was fortunate to have met her for the first time during her wedding. Yes, I officiated her wedding, no need to remind me of how old I am. Anyhow, we all sit and look at her pictures with deep sorrow. My heartfelt condolences go to every single one of you..."

The priest mumbled on, which infuriated me. I just wanted to get out of this bench and talk. Here I was forced to listen, until mum came to the stand. She took her time to settle in, fumbling papers around erratically and fidgeting the microphone to adjust the height.

"I WILL - "she distanced herself from the microphone a bit. "S-sorry. I will try to keep this short. I'm not very good with those sorts of things, so please bear with me."

"Ears up!" She continued. "That was one of her catchphrases; always seemingly strong, expecting us to be the same. Whenever we had something to say that went against her word, she would say 'no discussion'. That was all she had to do to get the message through. This was our Ela. With the love of a good swear word she would roam our lives without fear, and without beating around the bush. That is what you got – complete honesty, rather rare nowadays. I remember asking her about her opinion on a guy I dated, who now is my beloved husband. When I asked, she looked at me and said, 'he's ugly', and continued doing her crossword as if nothing happened," everyone laughed a bit.

"Yes, that is what she said. We laughed about it much later too, and Ela and my husband grew close over the years. I want to stress *how much* she loved her grandkids too. They became the world to her; a new kind of love that sparked a new chapter in her life. I would know because she told me that. I truly believe that she is up there, somewhere in heaven, smoking a cigarette and watching all of this. She wouldn't care about any expensive flowers, or grand gestures, I'm sure. All that matters to her is that you're here right now. I thank you all for being here and remembering her life together.

I love you mum, and I miss you dearly. Thank you."

Mum stepped down and kissed the casket. Four of my uncles and cousins heaved up the casket and walked out the church. Behind it, formed a long line. Me and dad were the first pair behind the casket. There was a small group of people standing outside the church. Among them was Ela's older brother, fixed onto a wheelchair. He wore a white suit and new brown shoes, that sat on the footrests of the wheelchair. He used his square pocket to wipe his tears, of which there were many. My dad left my side to push his wheelchair. When he caught up, grandpa said to me, "We can do this together." I didn't know what to do, so I gave him my hand. He squeezed it tightly.

The walk to the cemetery took longer than ever. Before it was just a minute from church, but then it felt like a lifetime. And to some degree it was. We all walked Ela to her next destination – a large opening in the earth between two other graves. We all flocked around it.

It was a hot day. I felt bad that I wanted to rush things so I could go home and lay down. With the soles of my shoes I grinded the dirt and sand, back and forth in a swiping motion. My shoulders felt heavy, and my knees gave in a little bit.

"Kale, are you alright?" Dad asked me.

"I'm not sure," as soon as he heard that he took my arm and we walked a couple of grave rows away.

"Don't worry, it happens sometimes." He stopped and pointed at a rock so I would sit down. Dad knelt towards me and spoke after a brief moment of silence. "I also want to get out of here. This place spooks me out of my mind."

I never thought dad to be afraid of something, or at least 'spooked'.

"Really?" I said.

"Yes, really. I just want to lay on my couch and watch TV like any other day. I would hear Marcelina talk through the phone with her friends. Mum would be right next to me under her orange blanket, worrying about you being alone upstairs."

"But I like it that way. It's too loud downstairs!" I laughed.

"Sorry, but I cannot watch my movies on silent," he joined in the laughter.

He quickly stopped though.

"It's not good to laugh during funerals, Kale. Either we can stay here, or we can go now and continue laughing," he jiggled the car keys in his pocket.

Even though I wanted to go badly, in the back of my head I knew this funeral wouldn't last too long anymore, and most importantly, it was a goodbye to Ela. I had to be strong for her.

"I will stay," I said.

"Alright then. I will give you a minute and I will see you there." He patted me on the back, grunting from standing up from his knees.

The rock wasn't comfortable at all, so I turned to face the grave in front of me to adjust myself. The grave said:

In loving memory

Mary Kristling

A mother full of heart &
the best wife in the world

and

Paul Kristling

The happiest man on earth.

Chapter Four

8 years later...

It had been eight years now. Since then, a lot had changed. Mum and dad separated, practically strangers. Marcelina lived with her boyfriend, and Ada was doing great in school. I decided to go to the local university. Somehow, I ended up doing a Life Science degree, living in my own apartment near the city centre. During my first two years I met many people, some of whom became good friends.

Nearly every day I went to the university library, which had an amazing park in front of it. It was always crammed by students, but it seemed to always have a place for another, no matter how full. One day, just after a biology class, I went out to finish up my assignments for the following day. This time I decided to go look for a café. I normally wouldn't drink coffee, but it started to grow on me.

The streets near campus were newly paved. Rivers of dark asphalt splitting buildings and greens. It doesn't matter where you'd go, every now and then a church or cemetery would greet you on your travels. Some older, some newer, but they always popped up in street corners. Always.

Just when I passed a cemetery, there was a little pathway beside it leading to a bushy gate. A sign stood in front of it:

Guine's Café
OPEN

I didn't know a lot of cafés, but what I did know was that mysterious gates next to aggressive rose bushes were very intriguing. Without any deeper consideration I walked over and pushed open the noisy gate. The hush of cars from the street was overpowered by the bustling outdoor section. Pockets of laughter in the crowd sitting on garden chairs. The patio was massive. It was surrounded by walls covered in moss and flowers. It was beautiful. When I closed the gate, a waitress spotted me.

"I'll get to you in a second," she zig-zagged between tables. I just waited there awkwardly till she came up to me.

"Welcome to Guine's café. Will it be a table for one?"

"Mhm, yep," I smiled.

"Very well. There are no places available outside, so I would have to seat you indoors, is that alright?"

"Mhm"

"Alrighty! Follow me." She turned around quickly, whipping her ponytail. It was difficult to keep up through the maze of the tables and chairs. I had to focus on her to not get lost or do anything stupid. "There you go. Do you want to order immediately, or do you want to scan the menu perhaps?"

She caught me off guard, I was still in full focus of following her.

"Ehm, sorry?"

She looked at me raising both hands slightly and weighing them up and down. "Menu, yes or no?"

"Yes, please."

"Awesome, be right back."

Then she whizzed away. I took off my bag and leaned it against the leg of the table. Just then did I have time to look around. It was gorgeous inside as well! A massive island filled with baristas, from which waitresses and waiters came and went all day. Little windows surrounded me, each with its own flowerpot. After I got the menu, I decided to order a cappuccino, with a white chocolate brownie. Even though I came just for coffee, the deserts were too tempting to ignore. I was happy I did because it was delicious. I got a big piece too!

I finished it in a heartbeat. The waitress saw me and came by.

"Already done?" She took the empty plate and cup.

"Yes, it was amazing thank you," I stood up grabbing my bag underneath the table.

"Already leaving? You just got here."

"I need to get some work done. This was supposed to be only a short stop on the way to the library."

"You can study here. The WIFI password is 'Gcafe454' "

"Thank you, but I don't want to take up this place."

"Oh, don't worry about that, many people are here since forever. You will be no trouble."

I froze, thinking about it intently.

"I guess I will stay then, thank you. Can you spell the password out for me again please?" I said.

"G-c-a-f-e-4-5-4. Can I get you anything else?"

I wrote it down quickly on my phone.

"I'm good for now, thank you so much."

"Great!" She then whipped her ponytail around again, proud of herself that she could persuade me to stay.

I was the only one on a laptop, which made me uneasy. I was saved by the work I had to do, into which I immersed myself fully.

The assignments were finished one after another, until I had nothing left to do than to pay and go home. The window revealed it to be drizzling, so I put my hood up while I made my way out.

"You got everything done?" The waitress caught me.

"Ah, yes. All done."

"It seemed you were very busy."

"Eh, yes, I was." There was an awkward silence after I said that.

"Looks like it's raining," she said.

"Oh, it's just a drizzle. Thanks for the coffee and brownie. Bye!"

I didn't want to hold her up.

I expected to get wet, but what I didn't expect was to get greeted with wind slamming my face just when I shut the door behind me. What a nice café that was, cheap too! Temporarily guided by the GPS on my phone to find a major street, I passed by a warehouse across the street from which bright light radiated. At the front stood a big pile of scrap metal – some of it was rusted too.

"Kale!" I heard someone shout from this very warehouse. After a more thorough scan, I saw a man stand in front of the pile wearing a grey onesie. He was camouflaged pretty well.

"Do I know you?" I said, trying to keep it short.

"Are you kidding?" He threw away his finished cigarette and jogged across the street.

"Ben? What are you doing here? I haven't heard from you for a while. How are you?" I gave him a hug.

"It's awesome to see you. Since graduation the class has scattered all over. From then on, I've been working here full time, as a welder."

"Oh, that's awesome. Do you like it?"

"It's not easy work I'll tell you that! But it's rewarding, and to be honest I didn't have any other plans anyway. What are you doing nowadays?" He said.

"I'm a Life Science student here at the university. Just coming back from Gaine's café."

"It's 'Guine's'," he laughed. "But Life Science! Wouldn't have thought you'd be brave enough. Good for you though, you like it?"

"Oh yes, I love it. It's so lovely to see - " I got interrupted by a loud metallic noise from the warehouse. A tall man in a onesie the same as Ben's shouted towards us.

"Ben, back to work!"

Ben looked at me with a little smirk and made his way back. "Nice to see you again, Kale. See you around."

When I came back to my senses, I felt wet all over. I must've forgotten it was raining. I speedwalked home and hung all my clothes to dry on the radiator.

I live in a small flat, and definitely not in the newest of buildings, but it was mine. Rather, I made it my own. It took quite a bit of work to fix the small things all around, retouching, repainting and so on. It was worth it though!

I was exhausted from all the work at the café, so I made myself some tea and soon enough dozed off into the oncoming evening.

I woke up without my alarm. The sun didn't peak through the curtains. Feeling energised I hurled myself up, surprised it was dark. My phone said 3:12 am. I must've fallen asleep very early. Not wanting to waste time needlessly laying in my bed, I made myself ready for the day. The plan was to clean up my flat, get some groceries, and meal prep for the next two to three days. To be honest, that was how it looked like most of the time – living alone wasn't the most exciting thing in the world. The house was cleaned, and all freshened up when the sun rose, and robins began screaming their heads off. They usually woke me up, as their nest was right next to my bedroom window, but not this time!

Our exams were in about two weeks' time, which would bring my third year of university to a close. To 'reward' completing part of my chores, I set out to study for those exams. Even though it was not till an hour later that all the buildings on campus opened, I just had to get out the house. I packed all my things, took a long proud look at all the empty shelves, wiped tables and neatly arranged things all around, and left.

It was still quite chilly, and the dew was covering the grass polished my shoes. As per usual, I took off with my headphones, because without my music I wouldn't dare to go anywhere. On my clueless walk towards campus, I witnessed the city waking up. Men in suits throwing their bags onto passenger seats, rushing to go to work. Kids with their puffy jackets holding hands with their mums, and on occasion their dads. A group of students passed by me, laughing and screaming just like the robins, wearing sunglasses and bucket hats, weaving in rhythm to the music of their speaker. When I reached the park in front of the library, I sat down on one of its benches. While I was waiting for the library to open, I looked through my notes to begin learning. At first, I was alone, but then there were two of us, then four, soon enough there was a whole group of students waiting.

I scrambled my notes together, stood up, and waited in line at the library doors, because I began to be cold. To my surprise I noticed one of my good friends to be there as well.

"Hey Roland! Roland!"

He turned around.

"Kale, what's up?" We shook hands. I and Roland have trained our handshake. It took us more than it should've, but we were proud to use it every time there was an opportunity. "You starting to worry about the exams, right?"

"Yeah, I don't have anything better to do right now. I need to absolutely smash that exam, so I can finish this year with a bang." I said.

"Sounds like a plan. What will you be studying specifically? Maybe we can sit together? I'm tired of being alone all the time, a study buddy would be amazing."

"Study buddy – yes that's sounds good. I'm going over chronologically from the first topic. That would be *Genes*." I answered.

"Alright, floor 5?" The library had books on different subjects depending on the floor you were on. Floor 5 was for Physics and Maths, but it had the most comfortable seats of any floor.

As soon as the staff opened the doors, we took our seats and immersed ourselves into our own miseries – with headphones on of course. We have learned from past experiences that studying without headphones tempted us to talk to each other. So often we wouldn't get anything done because of that.

Deep into our study session Roland tapped my hand, and pointed at his ear.

"- to go," I pulled out my headphones.

"What?"

"I need to go. Got class in 15 minutes. I got a lot done, thanks for sitting with me." We shook hands. "I meant to ask you, do you have any plans this weekend? We are throwing a small party."

"When is it exactly? I can come, but only Saturday," I said.

"Yes, it's on Saturday. Alright, just text me. I need to head off now." He quickly disappeared behind shelves of books.

To reassure myself I had time, I looked at my planner. Not only did my studying fill up a lot of my time, but I also started my part-time job in the local zoo. It was a huge one too, attracting many visitors.

I didn't stay much longer as well, I had my own lectures to attend to, which weren't that exciting as the practical ones. Till the weekend, I just studied, ate, and slept. I really wanted to do well on those exams. My goal was to try and graduate with the best grade I would be capable of getting. You know the phrase – leave no stone unturned. Yeah, that.

After long days, Saturday came around. I had a study session in the morning so I didn't feel too bad that I would waste my time during that party. Well, *waste* is a strong word. I knew it was good to turn off for a while. I dressed in a polo shirt and put gel in my hair. On my way there I stopped by a corner shop to buy something to drink. I had work the next day, so I bought some juice. I didn't like alcohol that much anyway. I didn't understand why everyone liked it so much. I tried it a couple times last year, gave in under peer pressure. Out of all of them, white wine was the best, but compared to non-alcoholic drinks it was average at best. One time Roland poured me a bit of Tequila to try out, I literally gagged – so horrible.

Anyway, I bought the juice and got to the party late. Music greeted me already from the pavement, and behind the closed blinds I could see shadows of people whizzing by from one side to the other.

The strong smell of weed was overwhelming, as well as the group of already drunk and high students at the front door that I had to squeeze through. By then I understood what I agreed to. The door flung open just as I wanted to grab the handle. I was met by high pitched screaming and hands flew in the air.

"Ahh! Kale, so nice to see you! Last time we were at a party together was a year ago, right?" She came in to hug me. Two of her friends just waited, smiling, filling up the doorway even more.

"Yeah, I guess."

"When Roland told me you agreed to come, I didn't believe him, but here you are! Meet my friends, this is Stephanie and Sara."

I never knew, in these moments, whether I was supposed to go for a hug, or just a handshake. I didn't feel too keen, so I just shook their hands.

"Kale, nice to meet you – Hi, nice to meet you."

"Let's go, they are waiting for us outside, Ellie" Stephanie said. "See you around Kale."

When I finally made it in. On every stable surface there were glass bottles, cans and cups. I had to strain myself to find some snacks. I took out my jug of apple juice and put the straw in it. I couldn't be bothered with cups anymore.

People I never saw before looked at me and laughed. I just minded my own business, or at least I tried. To not stand there like some weirdo, I tried to find a group of friends. I found some guy puking into the kitchen sink. Maybe not him. While I walked around I kept hearing snippets of gossip from multiple groups. That wasn't what I was looking for either. Heading upstairs I finally found Roland. He was on the second floor smoking out the window.

"Hey Roland! I was looking for you." I said.

I startled him. "Gosh, don't jump at me like that. Come here." We shook hands. "What have you been drinking? You look sober."

I lifted my jug. He looked confused, but after his cogs finished turning, he laughed out loud. He took a puff of his cigarette and looked out again.

"Why did you come so late, Kale?"

"I had some chores to do."

"The night will be long, so I guess it doesn't matter much. It's really getting started just about now, everyone has reached their cruising state -." Just as he said that a guy fell into the bush of the front yard. "- or landing state".

"Are you alright?" I asked.

"D-don't listen to me, the weed is kicking off and I just needed some fresh air. Make yourself at home. You can leave your jacket in my room."

I would if I had taken one with me.

I went down again, sitting on the only free armchair available around the living room table. To the left of me was a group of girls standing around with cups in their hands, slowly moving from side to side in rhythm with the music. On the other side of the table was another group. They were discussing the layout of the university lectures and how unproductive it was. They saw that I was listening, and kindly invited me to the conversation.

"What do you think about your courses?"

"I'm not a fan of theory, but I guess it is necessary. I much rather do practice."

"Practice?" they looked confused. "What degree are you doing?"

"Life Sciences. 40 percent of our lectures are practice where we do all sorts of things really. We are learning about living organisms after all."

"Oh, you're lucky. We all do *real* science here, like Chemistry and Physics - " After a long while of nodding, I got saved by a girl to my right side.

"Difficult, isn't it?"

"Hmmm?" I turned to her.

"Difficult to not get offended by them. Don't worry, you're not the only one."

It was Trina, Roland's girlfriend.

"I'm glad to see you, I don't know a lot of people here."

"You know us, we like to invite all kinds of people. I don't know many of them as well, but I hope Roland does," she said. "Speaking of him, he is probably out somewhere having the time of his life with his pals."

I wasn't sure whether to tell her that he was upstairs all by himself. It didn't seem he wanted company, so I just played dumb. I followed her into the kitchen because she wanted to make herself a drink.

"What are you drinking over there?"

"Apple juice, you want some?"

"No thanks, I need something strong. The exams are coming up and I need help to relax a bit."

Just from watching her mixing this mean drink I started to feel sick, so I just looked elsewhere and found something better to look at. Some guy was dancing to the music rather recklessly. It was funny to see everyone staring and enjoying his freedom. It wasn't difficult to spot that he didn't care, he was just doing what felt right. He was so interesting that for a long while I and Trina watched him, tapping our feet in rhythm.

A new song started; Trina pulled my sleeve and demanded we danced. Gosh, I knew this would come someday. It was incredibly embarrassing for me to admit it, but I couldn't dance. I always got out of such situations before. I tried ignoring her at first, making it seem like I didn't hear her, but she pulled again.

"Come on, let's dance," she said again, this time louder.

"No thanks."

"I really like this song, don't be like that and come dance."
She gave out an honest smile, which I couldn't say no to.

We placed ourselves next to the guy we stared at and
shuffled in place. I focused my gaze on her, so I didn't have to
see people looking at me.

She flung her hair left to right, right to left and waved her
arms around lively. Through her flying hair I could see she had
her eyes closed, not hiding behind a pair of glasses anymore.
For a while I sort of swayed from side to side, until she looked
at me. Her facial expression was one of confusion, but gratitude.

"I'll help you," she said.

She took both of my hands and swung them.

"Look! You have to put your foot here – yes there! And
then you pull me in to your chest and out again – very good!
Let's try again, but don't pull that hard," she giggled.

One of the reasons I couldn't dance was that I lacked the
ability of being delicate. I couldn't do smooth motions, so what
Trina asked of me was near impossible to do. We did the same
move over and over again, until I memorized all the steps.

"Between these steps you can just do whatever you feel
like," she said.

"- How?"

"You're too focused on everything. Instead of thinking,
try to feel." She then put her hand in front of my eyes, blocking
all my vision. "What are you focusing on now?"

"Where I am." I stretched my arms in order to feel around
me.

"Try to listen and not to see," she let her hand go.

I tried to do what she asked, not only because I was
curious, but also… why not?

I closed my eyes and listened to the music intently. I could
hear the drums, the guitar, and a keyboard. I wasn't sure about
the last one. I knew that song quite well, but never did I really

listen. Music was always there, whatever I did, but it was in the background. Never did I pay any greater attention to it until now. And just when I came back from this thought I could feel my feet moving and my head bouncing.

"I can feel it," I said to Trina.

"Me too! Look how much you have improved!" She said.

When I opened my eyes, I saw her looking at my feet.

"Now, let's try this move right here..."

For the rest of the party, we practiced our dance skills. Well, I did the practicing, she did more of the showing. For the first time of my life, I had fun dancing in front of other people. The night ended when people started to disappear, and I grew too tired to move another muscle. When I headed home Trina was still going strong. She really inspired me that night.

I opened my eyes to see the robins screaming in front of my window. When I pulled my arm out of my cocoon, I grunted out loud. The pain woke me up immediately. I couldn't get up, everything felt sore, but I knew I slept well. The morning routine wasn't as pleasant as it used to be, hurling my zombie body from room to room, getting ready for work.

My commute ended at the gates of the zoo, which was right across the city theatre. I felt so at peace when I saw my little ones. I was taking care of butterflies in a butterfly house. It was kind of like a dome greenhouse, but with butterflies in it and loads of plants. It was magnificent.

I was still learning my way around this place, that was why during my shift a veteran was helping me. He was a tall, well-built man in his 50s. He wore round glasses that fit his well-defined face.

"Kale! Good morning to you!" He stood up from his office chair.

"To you too, Anthony. Please let me know the reason behind your infectious smile!" We shook hands.

"We received new eggs," pointing towards a pile of special boxes. "But on a sadder note, I saw some *reds* dead on the ground. We need to get to them today."

By *reds* Anthony meant a butterfly species called 'Red admiral'. It was mostly black, but had striking red spots or lines. It was one of our favourites, even though we love all our beauties. Besides caring for butterflies, we also bred some chosen species that could be found in the wild.

After some checking and paperwork, we set off to work. Anthony, being the professional, mostly inspected the butterflies, while I kept an eye on the plants. The most important thing was to identify whether a disease had befallen a given plant. If so, it had to be removed as soon as possible, so it the disease wouldn't spread. After inspecting all the plants and caring for them, I joined Anthony so he could teach me new things.

"Rough day *son*?" He asked me when I came back to our office in full sweat.

"Yeah, I was at a party yesterday, all the dancing gave me a good kick in the butt."

Anthony burst out laughing. All I could do was sink into my chair and frown at him.

"I didn't expect you to be a dancer. Gun to my head I would guess you would be the 'sitting and staring' type."

"Very funny," I swiped the dirt off my knees.

"Care for a drink?"

"Yes, please. The juice I brought today is on the top shelf," I said.

Anthony opened the fridge. "The mixed fruit one? Or do you mean the orange one?"

"Mixed fruit please. The orange one is for later."

"Yes, sir."

I leaned back and let the juice relieve me from my pain.

"Lucky for you my friend, we don't have a lot to do. I already took care of most things. I waited for you to join me so we can go inspect the wood whites."

"Mhm…"

"I will give you some time to recover. I'll head out for some fresh air."

Anthony was ambitious and always found some work to do, but he was able to see when it was enough. It took me a while to gather my energy for Anthony's lecture. Shortly after noon my shift ended, and, just like my juice bottles, I left completely empty. I wasn't a big fan of naps, but you bet I took one.

I spent the rest of the day resting and going in and out of naps, until I was befallen by deep sleep when I dreamed:

I'm in the clouds. Everything I see is blurry. It was dark, yet occasional sunrays shone through, blinding me. Looking up, I could see the blue, curved outline of the horizon. Then all of the sudden I rushed down through the clouds – I was falling. When the sky cleared I could see everything – the plains, the forests, the rivers and lakes, and the villages and cities. I was going faster and faster towards the side of a city, until I hit the glistening dome of a church. Then all went dark, but I saw the sun anew.

It was Monday, and so the week began yet again. In the back of my mind I had those pesky exams, but I didn't have the will to go to the library. So, I continued lying in bed for longer than usual. I didn't have lectures on Mondays so I could potentially stay in for the day. Before noon, all I did was eat breakfast and watch a few episodes of a series.

When the credits rolled, I felt sleepy again, so I decided to make myself a coffee. I held the coffee beans in my hand when I remembered the café I went to the other day. I drooled over the brownie.

In a heartbeat I was out the house, making a beeline to the café. It didn't take long to see myself eating that brownie. It was just what I needed. This time I was sitting outside right next to the mossy wall that surrounded the place. Luckily, my laptop automatically connected to the Wi-Fi because I forgot the password.

I was reading an enticing article about some fan theory concerning the series I watched, when out of nowhere someone stood in front of me.

"Studying again, are we?"

It was the waitress from last time. She startled me and I nearly pushed the little plates over the edge. I didn't want to tell her the truth, so I just made up something on the spot.

"Eh, yes."

"What about?" she said.

"Butterflies and how to breed them."

"Oh wow, that's a hobby I never heard of", she laughed.

"It's – yeah. It's complicated stuff."

"Can I see?" She walked around me to see the screen. I took evasive action and out of instinct slammed the laptop shut. She looked at me in an irritated manner.

"No." That's all I could think of.

"Why not?"

"It's a secret."

"It's a secret? – about butterflies?" she looked irritated.

"Precisely."

She gave up on the conversation and headed back. Feeling terrible, I said to her loudly, "I want you to see them in person, and not just on a screen."

She turned around, revealing a smile.

Out of fear that she would come again, I packed my laptop and finished my coffee without anything else than my wandering thoughts. I still felt incredibly stressed out by that encounter and cringed at my own behaviour. Repetitive thoughts about that awkward interaction ravaged in me. At least I was lucky enough that when I went in to pay, I didn't cross paths with her again. I had no idea how I would handle that.

Afterwards, I went to the library for some time, as I was already out the house. In the evening I finished reading the fan theories, while I blasted some music.

I had a lecture the next day, in the afternoon. It was in one of the main halls on campus. The buildings surround a large open space, on which students liked to sit and relax when the weather was great. Today wasn't an exception.

I entered the hall, and it was nearly full. Even though I saw the same students in every lecture, I still thought I was seeing the faces for the first time. But in the sea of strangers, I always found a familiar face that I could sit next to.

"Hey Roland. All good?"

"Yeah, I'm a bit sick after Saturday."

I could see the people sitting around us eavesdropping.

"Oh, that's too bad. Drinking tea helps a ton. Thank you for leaving this seat free by the way," I said.

"Yeah, I will not drink that crap. I will stick to water thank you very much. I see your juice has served you well."

"It has! I feel great, but yesterday I had such an awkward situation. I will tell you later."

Roland gave me the curious eye, but I persisted to tell him after the lecture. To no one's surprise I forgot all about it. In the hall you could see many tired faces and towards the back rows some were sleeping. Our professor was strict, but turned a blind eye to us as she knew that the exams started next week.

As I walked back home from campus, the dream I had popped back into my mind. It was rare for me to dream so vividly. I didn't think too much of it, but I enjoyed the picturesque nature. Consequently, I thought back to my encounter with my old friend Ben at the welding place. I looked him up on social media and was surprised that I still had him in my friends list. It took me longer than it should have to figure out what to write, since the last time we wrote was back in middle school.

We had arranged to meet up at a bar that Ben usually went to. His texting style was very direct and straight to the point. Quite efficient.

Walking there, I could finally see the bar Ben meant. Its sign on top was rusty and close to unreadable. The painted wooden pillars flaked, and the corners of the windows were covered in some sort of black tar. The door wasn't better either, it screeched loudly when I swung it open. A room full of judging faces greeted me uneasily. I walked to the first free table I found, looking at the floor constantly. It was a bustling place, but small enough to hear the individual conversations being held. It stank of alcohol and unhygienic people. I know it's rude to say it like that, but you know what I mean – the acidic smell you get when someone hasn't washed for a while, with dirt under their long fingernails, worn clothing rubbing against their sweaty skin, and an oily whirl of hair. Despite these unwelcoming features, it still didn't break my excitement to see Ben again. I waited for him because he said something about eating together. My stomach grumbled, so I decided to order something to drink. The bartender was the only woman in the bar.

I squeezed between two gentlemen to get to the cash register.

"Could I get one glass of orange juice please?" I said to the lady.

"Come again?" She came closer.

I repeated myself and she looked at the men beside me and smiled. I heard a deep scoff from both sides.

"We don't serve juice here. If you want something non-alcoholic, I can get you some water. Free of charge of course," she pointed at the tap. "We also have tea and coffee if you prefer."

"Water please."

"Sure, honey."

I went back to the table still only looking at the floor. I nearly finished the glass when Ben finally arrived. He wore a leather jacket, loose jeans and three rings on both hands which gleamed similarly to his finely combed hair. He flicked his hand up and demanded a beer on the way to me.

"Hello Kale. Your invitation was a nice surprise," he sat down after a firm handshake. I was glad he managed to come.

"What you drinking there?"

"Water," I said.

"Water?"

"Yeah, I wanted juice, but they don't have any."

He laughed out loud. "You serious?" He leaned back toward the bar and shouted across the room: "Make it two *will ya?*" He turned back to me, "You will like this beer here, just give it a try. Don't worry it's on me."

"Thanks," I mumbled.

"So how you holding up? Sorry about the interruption last time, my boss is a real *ass.*"

"I'm all good. I thought about you and wanted to continue the conversation," I said.

"How cute of you. I'm good too, just work is breaking my balls, you know. It's horrible, but you need to pay the beer with something, am I right?"

Just when he said that the bartender showed up to our table with two pints. "You're exactly right Ben," she said. "He thinks he is all so clever; don't believe everything he says. He is a sly fox," she looked at me.

"Come on! Don't do me like that in front of my old friend here," he leaned back surprised.

"You'll thank me later," she winked at me. "So, boys, what do you want to eat?"

I didn't know what they offered so I let Ben go first.

"I will have the usual, with extra cheese. It's Kale's first time here, so he must try some of your chicken soup with the *schnitzel.*"

The lady nodded and made her way back to the counter, where a couple guests waited for some service. I was annoyed that Ben ordered for me, mostly because I actually wanted something else.

"About your job – " I continued our conversation "- what exactly are you welding?"

"Everything really. Whatever comes up, but mostly I'm welding old train wagon parts so they can be used again. We are situated close to the train tracks after all, so it is quite convenient."

Engineering, and physics for that matter, always seemed a mystery to me. I was tragic in that subject in school.

"Do you know the difference between a good and a bad weld?" he asked me.

"No, not really."

"Me neither!" He laughed. "I just do it until the pieces stick together. I'm the only certified welder there, so they don't know either."

I was simultaneously surprised and not surprised. Just to think how many pieces Ben welded incorrectly. I just hoped it was a joke. In the meantime, the waitress silently brought me the soup, which I started to eat quickly.

"Doesn't it bother you?" I asked slurping the hot soup.

"What do you mean?"

"To not know whether you do a good job or not," I said.

"Not really. It's a job after all. In school we were checked non-stop with all those tests and stuff. I wanted to take life into my own hands and control whatever I can. At work I'm the master, you know what I mean?"

He looked around nervously the whole time, like he was on edge. It made me anxious, but I tried to keep my cool. "And how's your family?" I tried to change the topic.

"I don't know, and who gives a damn? We are not on good terms now. There are many things in play, but in short: I wanted to do things and my family wanted me to do other things. Now all I have is a girlfriend and a small child – little kiddo called Sarah."

"Congratulations!" I lifted my glass in order to toast, but he didn't budge. Rather awkwardly I just drank a bit of the bitter beer. "To your girlfriend, Sarah, and an impeccable taste of beer!" I said barely swallowing it without wincing.

"It's good, isn't it?" He smiled, but looked elsewhere, distracted.

An awkward silence followed, where I took another big sip of beer, trying to figure out what the next topic should be.

"Kale, you remember the incident when we were kids?" He beat me to the punch.

"Hmm?"

"You know, the incident in the park," he said.

"Oh, yeah of course I remember. It became a legend in school, so it would be difficult to forget. I'm sure everyone else would still know."

He frowned at me. "I'm glad" he said sarcastically, taking his first sip of his beer. "You know, it damn sure hurt, but that's beside the point. Do you remember who did it?"

I had to think for a while.

"I will help you," Ben said. "It was goddamn Henrik."

I nodded, as he continued.

"Henrik, that bastard. He really got me good there. One moment I see the ball and him, the next I wake up in the hospital with my mother beside me. Do you know what hurt the most?"

"To see your mother see you –", he interrupted me. I quickly took yet another sip, embarrassed that I didn't notice that it was rhetorical.

"He disappeared. No apology, no explanation... nothing. Boys fight, I understand that, sometimes it gets serious, but you always own up, you know what I mean? Then, *years* later, I see that asshole on the street. What would you do?"

"I'm not sure. I can't imagine that scenario, but probably I would just ignore him and do my thing."

"Ignore? Are you sure? Because I got the hankering to beat that guy up, just as he did to me," he said.

"Sounds to me like you're looking for an *excuse* to beat him up. If he would 'own up', as you said, you would still find something wrong in him to beat him up for."

"I'm not looking for excuses Kale!" He slammed the table with his fist. "I just want some payback at least. He is walking around all happy and *shit*. I swear, next time I see him I will knock him out."

I just wanted to leave at this moment. On the way home there was a fast food restaurant I could go to. However, I didn't find the courage to tell him, so I just sat there like a stick in the mud and nodded at everything he said. He went on and on about Henrik. I stopped listening to him and got lost in my own thoughts, until the waitress came back with the food.

" – how dare he – "

"Alright guys here it is! The schnitzel for you and the burger for you." She planted the plates in front of us, taking my empty soup plate. "Did you like it?".

"Yes, it was very good!" I showed her a thumbs up, managing to squeeze out a sincere smile to make her happy.

"If you need anything don't be shy," she said proudly.

"Yeah, we know that." Ben said to her, immediately taking a bite of the burger.

The schnitzel looked hot, so I waited. Ben on the other hand ate half his burger already. All I could do was watch him devour it, smacking, slurping, and aggressively licking his lips. His wife needed to be a patient woman.

"You not hungry?" He said quickly with a full mouth. I could see little pieces of burger being spat out onto the table as he did so.

"It's hot," I replied.

"Mhm," he started his fries, eating five at a time.

"You were hungry, weren't you?" I said.

"Mhm"

He finished his meal as if it was a race, gulping down the rest of his beer.

"Oh man that was good," he was still licking his lips. "I'll go take a piss, hold on for a moment, *will ya?*"

I was delighted to hear it. Finally, a break to take off my mask. I could eye roll and mumble out my frustration. Plus, I could start eating in peace.

Ben came back as I was halfway through the meal. He still looked on edge, seeming to tip toe wherever he went, twisting his head often to look around. It made me nervous, and I could see the older couple in front of us were too.

"How you like it? All good?" He leaned on the table.

"Yeah, it's pretty go-"

"Nice, I'm going to go for a cigarette, is that alright with you?"

I didn't even have to respond to that, he was already on his way to the door anyway. I got more time for myself, which seemed to be worth a lot.

I finished my meal and after a couple sips finished the beer as well. The waitress saw me finish and came up to me taking the glasses and plates. I thanked her and all she did was smile and say "sure honey" in her rough voice.

I felt full and started to yawn, but still wanted something sweet to complete the meal. To stretch out a bit, I went to the toilet. I came back sitting down at our table. I expected Ben to be back by now. He was probably talking with someone. I waited five minutes, then ten. When half an hour passed, I stood up and looked outside. I couldn't see anyone. I checked my phone, also nothing. I called him, but he didn't pick up. I went to the bar to sit at the counter.

"Everything alright? You look troubled," the woman said to me.

"Well, I can't find Ben."

"I know. I heard you were old friends. I wanted to say something, but I thought it would be best for you to learn who he is by yourself. I don't know what he was like before, but he hasn't become a saint."

I put my phone back into my pocket and paid for everything.

"Thanks hon. Can I get anything else? It will be on the house. A tea or coffee perhaps, I saw you yawning back there."

"What tea do you have?"

"Too many to remember. Shoot me with a flavour and I will say whether we have it."

"Lavender?"

"Let's see." She opened a shelf under the counter. From the reflection on a fridge standing behind her I could see that the shelf was indeed filled with loads of tea boxes. She rummaged in it for a while, taking out everything sitting at the front.

"Gotcha," she said reaching deep. "It will be just a moment." She quickly put all the tea boxes back and turned on the kettle. "How do you know Ben exactly?"

"We went to school together till end of middle school. Then we went our own ways."

"Hold on, so that would be more than five years ago, surely."

"More, but yeah, long time."

"Don't worry, he really isn't worth it anymore. I saw him a lot before, but now he isn't coming all too often." She took a sip of a beer she poured out for herself. "Shows that people can change, not only for the better, but also for the worse. I had a similar experience as you just did. I found that the fact that they've become the new person isn't the problem. The problem is that we've expected that nothing has changed."

She was right. I had nothing to add to that. My phone vibrated in my pocket, so I took it out. The waitress went to serve other people.

Trina wrote to me. She invited me once more to theirs, no party this time though. I accepted the invite. They asked me over quite often, to chat and play some games, but because of the exams and all that, it became more infrequent.

"Your girlfriend?" the waitress came back, pointing at my phone in my hand.

"What?" I said confused, trying to connect the dots. "Oh!

111

No, my friends asked me to hangout."

"I saw you smiling from ear to ear, so I thought it must be someone special." She slid my tea over to me. "Enjoy."

"Thank you."

I waited quite a long time for the tea to cool. But once it did, I chugged it and made my way home. "Why did he do that?" I asked myself about Ben. I wasn't even angry; I was just disappointed and confused. At least I ate something, I didn't completely waste my time. On my way I spotted a bakery, and through the glass I saw so many tempting goodies that I had to buy something. I convinced myself I deserved it somehow. Little did I know that I would overdo it. I left having bought six doughnuts and cakes. Stepping out of the bakery I realised that it started raining. I thought I would make it home before it would get any worse, but the rain really took off. To shelter my paper-wrapped goodies, I took refuge in front of an entrance of a church.

The rain splashing on concrete and grass was one of my favourite sounds. To let time pass by quicker I listened intently and started eating a chocolate filled doughnut. Not much later the wooden door that was cracked open the whole time opened further.

"Oh sure, I'll do that. Greet Emma from me, will you? Goodbye!" An older woman in a coat appeared. "Oh goodness!" she looked at me and the rain. "Always ready for anything," she glanced at me, opening an umbrella which she took out of her deep coat pockets.

By this point I was already two doughnuts in, and felt sugar cover half my cheeks. I quickly swiped my face and hid the empty wrappers. And good that I did, a whole group followed her out the church. People of all ages, some kids as well, mostly dressed in elegant wear. I just minded my own business, looking into the distance, but checking out the people.

"Brownie boy?"

Damnit.

"Is that you?" I heard. "It is you, isn't it?"

I turned to see the waitress from Guine's café. It felt weird to see her out of her work clothes. Still all in black, but stylish.

"Oh hi! Just sheltering from the rain," I forced out a giggle.

"I see. Don't you want to go inside? We are finished now, and it is still open."

"Nah, I'm good," I waved my hand.

"It's so warm and cosy there, but suit yourself." She then pointed at the pile of wrappers and said, "Hungry?"

"Yeah, it was a moment of weakness on my part. Do you want some?"

"No, I'm good. I'm going to a restaurant to eat with my grandparents. Actually, I see they are waiting for me. I need to get going." She waved me goodbye and quickstepped towards them.

I ate for a bit longer, until I couldn't look at the sugar anymore. I ate two doughnuts and a bag of chocolate balls. I could've had a bit of a sugar problem. Anyway, by that time the rain had settled down somewhat. I took all the remaining wrappers into my hands and wanted to leave, but something bugged me. The door to the church was still cracked open, and something inside me told me to enter. I already gave in to temptation once, I might as well go for it the second time, I thought.

I stepped in silently, but the old wooden door gave me away. The sudden warmth overwhelmed me. I made sure to shut the door, so it wouldn't escape. The rustling of the wrappers echoed around the walls and the high ceilings that were covered in a simple triangular pattern. I counted fourteen in one row, and it was filled with them. My shoes were loud too, but I couldn't do anything about it.

There were a lot of decorations around to feast my eyes upon, but what took my breath away was the cross in the centre, behind the altar. It hung on two cables suspended from the ceiling, and Jesus hung with it. A few steps behind it – the wall was covered with little angels and prophets and the common people. The benches were old, but the dome in the centre was even older, reaching for the highest point of the church.

Looking up, fixing my gaze on such a high point gave me vertigo, so I snapped out of it. "I need to go home," I said to myself, fidgeting my keys in my pocket.

When I stood by the door, I heard a voice call to me.

"It was nice to see you again."

It was a priest that stood just in front of the massive cross. I had never seen him before, so I just nodded and closed the door behind me.

Sunrays blasted my face and puddles all around glistened. I didn't have to hold my deserts so tightly any longer. I made it home completely dry by some miracle.

Chapter Five

I couldn't get her out of my head, so it was the first time that I wanted to go to the café because of her, rather than the coffee. Yes, it was delicious, but something about that waitress intrigued me. It was a rather weird feeling, like an urge to scratch an itch.

Even though I had no reason, I brought my laptop with me and the usual notebooks. I put gel in my hair, swiping it to the side rather tightly. I put on a semi-casual shirt, contrasting it with a dark watch and leather boots.

I stepped out of my apartment in a rush, even though I had all the time in the world. I turned the keys, and took a step only for my foot to slide away. I quickly grabbed the radiator beside me not to fall. I slammed my ankle against it though.

"Uuggghh!" I tried to suppress it.

I stood there for a second for the pain to cease, realising that the neighbours have just cleaned the floor. Having hit the wall with my closed fist in frustration I went out to be greeted once more by the ordinary annoyance of day-to-day life: I forgot my wallet.

So, I went back inside, grabbed it and walked out carefully and cautiously. It was still slippery, even though I was much less erratic. I bet it was these leather shoes that didn't have any groves on the soles. Anyhow, I was *finally* going out of my damn building. All pumped up by rage I long-stepped my way to the tight alley with the gate at the end. Opening the ever so squeaky gate, it never ceased to amaze me how much of a shift in atmosphere and noise there was.

"Hi there. A table for one, or do you expect company?" A tall waiter came up to me near instantly. He must've seen me from afar.

"Could I have a table for two perhaps? There is a chance a friend of mine will come," I said.

"Sure, no biggie. Inside or outside?"

"Let's do inside please."

He turned quickly and near to sprinted in, just like the waitress used to do. I wondered whether they were just being funny, or if they legitimately learned this during training. I found it interesting the first time, but now it got annoying. That was why I followed him sluggishly, so he was forced to wait for me around corners and such. I giggled to myself because *I* had the upper hand this time.

"Here you go…" he placed the menu in my hands before I took the seat. "I will come back in a couple minutes. I recommend the –"

"A large cappuccino with the white chocolate brownie please," I smiled at him, giving the menu back.

He smiled back and stormed off into the sunset. At least that was what I imagined he did.

I turned left and right to glance whether I could see her amidst all the other people, but to no avail. I continued tapping my right leg up and down, looking around again and again. The seat in front of me accompanied me in this weird thing I have buried myself in. I hurled my backpack onto it because I thought I would feel less awkward.

Just as the waiter came with his hands full, I stood up and excused myself. He didn't seem to care really, as he was sure I wouldn't just leave.

I took so long fixing my hair that when I went back to my table and felt my cup of coffee, it wasn't hot anymore – lukewarm just as I liked it.

"Perfect timing," I said to myself. It was rare for me to take myself out without a real purpose. Usually, I just stayed in my flat. As I sipped my coffee, a TV a few tables to the left got my attention. It showed a football game. I was a big fan when I was younger, but I grew out of it. I had a feeling that it was all the same over and over. There were exciting moments, no doubt, but they were far too rare for me to be kept interested. I only watched it when Roland invited me to watch his favourite team.

I tried hard to figure out who was playing, but I couldn't make it out. The team names displayed were cut short to 'SHM' and 'TUN'. There were players dressed in yellow and players dressed in a weird mix of white and purple. They passed the ball side to side without real commitment to attack. When I looked around the café, I wasn't surprised to find that no one was watching. It was what we called a 'dead' game. Also, they were playing in the middle of the day. That was usually a sign of smaller clubs playing, or less important games.

As nothing was going on I decided to keep my laptop in my bag for a while and analysed the referee - watching him intently where he looked, where he ran to, and what his calls were. It was far more interesting of a job in my opinion than a footballer, but my younger self, as well as many others, would scold me for saying that.

The brownie was good as ever, but sadly my palate got used to the taste. It wasn't that 'shockingly' delicious. I wondered whether it was because I knew what it tasted like and held such a high expectation. The thought of having to stop myself eating it for a while didn't go well in my mind.

I looked around again to see if I could see her, but no. Two young women worked the registers and made the coffee, and two waiters were doing the deliveries to the tables. I wasn't happy, so I decided to open my laptop and notebooks to distract myself. It did work for some time. I tried to do Sudoku's as well. I had that thing where specific places made me wait in different manners. In waiting rooms, I did crossword puzzles, in airports I did word searches, and usually in buses I did Sudokus. I managed to finish one, but it felt weird not being in a bus while doing it, so I stopped. In my bag I also had a poetry collection by an amateur writer called "Split". I liked to read poetry in the library between my work for cooling off. With no other options I decided to leave, which was then when I had to ponder over the failure of meeting the waitress.

I went to pay at the register.

"Cash or card?" One of the women approached me. The person who chose who to employ for staff did a real good job. They seemed so relaxed and confident.

"Card," I responded. When she tapped the screen to put on the amount to the card reader, I just asked about her coworker.

"Do you know all your coworkers?"

She looked at me confused. I wasn't sure how to ask about the waitress I was looking for, but in hindsight that was not the best question to ask at first.

"I would surely hope so."

"Well, I was looking for someone who works here, and I was hoping to meet them again."

"Oh, what's the name?"

Damn, I had no clue.

"I don't know the name. She has black hair and is around this tall," I held my hand to a rough estimate of what I remembered.

"Ehm, that could be either Hanna, Susanne or Aysha." She offered me the card reader to pay.

That was something I didn't expect. At least I had her name down to three. I paid and then left after thanking and tipping her.

At least I had done a bit of work, I thought. To not waste the gel and all the preparation to get out the house I was thinking where to go. The park would be a waste of time, the café was already ticked off, the library wouldn't do the trick… Come to think of it, there weren't many places I could've went to. Roland thought of me as a 'sad human being' for only being in a handful of places in a repetitive cycle… Roland!

I texted him asking what he was doing, and he responded that he was in his house doing 'literally nothing'. He suggested to go to the cinema to see a movie. That wasn't a bad idea I thought. Last time I went there was an awkward one. I went with my family when I was around fourteen at the time. Ada wasn't with us as she was too young still. Mum and Marcelina went somewhere leaving me and dad alone. We went to get the tickets and I was ordering some popcorn and drinks. There was a girl a little older than me working there. All was good, until my dad said something along the lines of: 'You go son, remember what I told you.' Pushed me slightly forward towards the girl and stormed off. The look on her face… I remembered it for a long time. I didn't say anything, and afterwards he told me that I was so red that he though I'd pass out. He told me to

119

relax when talking to girls, but he always got a kick out of making things weird. Thinking of him made me miss him, and I chuckled thinking of that memory. Since then, I never stepped foot into the cinema again.

We reserved seats for 7pm today. A movie called 'Far and Forever'. Quick research told me it was set in a world where humans could teleport anywhere by putting in coordinates on a machine. The main character messed up the code and got teleported to another world. Thinking of those premises gave me an eerie nerve.

All that aside, it still didn't solve my problem. 7pm was still a long way away. I checked my account balance on my phone and calculated that I had some money to spare. I figured I could take myself out for lunch for the first time ever. But first I needed to get hungry, so I took a bus to visit the local beach. It was nearly an hour away, but what else would I do. My music and watching some silly videos on my phone made the bus ride much more comfortable.

Stepping out at the bus stop, the sun glared down with all the clouds in the sky floating away from it. The beach looked exactly like it did the last time I was there during my first year. I walked along it slowly, making sure to use the pavement and wooden boardwalks in order to keep my leather shoes intact. The waves made sure to cool me down by splashing hard against the small seawall, sprinkling me with refreshing winds.

I sat down on a bench on the boardwalk, which was behind a little hill, that was just big enough to provide for shade. My gel dripped down my forehead together with my sweat. I put my bag beside me and just watched the waves. Breaking the horizon were a few ships, seemingly motionless, but always on the move. Between me and them were its bow waves, eventually syncing with the gentle brushes of the sea. The short sand beach was struck by water even during low tides. Then there was me on the wooden platforms built a generation or two ago, kept up by its high convenience for jogging, soul searching, or just pure old loitering.

It was past midday once I grew bored of the pit of my meandering mind. To get out of the philosophy, I rang up Ada.

"What happened?" she said.

"What - nothing, nothing."

I could hear her sigh.

"Don't do such a thing! You never call, and when somebody like you calls, something tragic has happened."

"I'm sorry, I guess I just wanted to hear your voice," I said.

"That is nice to hear, I haven't heard yours too, it's weird, but nice. You know what I mean?"

"Yeah. Well, what you up to?"

"I'm studying now. Mum told me to work hard so I can get to a good middle school."

"Oh yes! I forgot you're in your final year. Time goes fast, I guess. Speaking of mum, how is she doing?"

"She is alright, just a bit tired and overworked. The gardening thing she's doing isn't easy on her, but she said it is fun."

"Ah, I see." I said. Mum worked full time and usually did overtime to make sure her and Ada were living well. Whenever I came to visit, mum was rarely there, and when she was, she was so tired she just wanted to go to sleep or relax. I felt bad for Ada that she had to be raised like this, but there wasn't a lot anyone could do. "What did mum say about you visiting me?" I continued.

"Oh, she said it was a great idea, but only after my exams."

"After mine too," we both laughed.

I could hear some shuffling noise for a while.

"I still have the birthday present you gave me in the bubbly paper thing," she said. "I'm scared to break it."

I gave her a globe with a real, preserved butterfly in it. Anthony helped me to get it done, it was his idea in the first place! We waited till one of our Red Admirals died to preserve it. It was a long wait, but we got it done.

"Don't worry, just make sure it sits on a desk, somewhere far from the edge. But if you want to keep it in the bubble wrap then you can do that too."

"Okay!"

A dog and its owner passed by me. The dog barked at another one down the path.

"You have a dog!!" she shouted in excitement.

"No, no. I'm just outside... at the beach."

"Is it cute? What kind of dog is it? Is it fluffy? What colour-"

She went on and on. We continued talking about dogs for a long while, but I didn't mind. We stopped the call when my bus arrived at the bus stop, as I had to go to eat if I wanted to manage in time for the movie.

I sat down in the bus next to the large window. In front of me sat a child and her dad. Naturally I had my headphones on, so I couldn't understand what they were constantly talking about. I kept looking out at the fields and greenery until I noticed the child pointing at me and facing the dad. I thought something was wrong so I took one of my headphones off.

I missed what the child was saying, but the dad responded.

"Oh, I'm sorry, it's nothing. She was just wondering why you were smiling."

"You're happy!" She pointed again, looking at me this time.

"Yes, I think I am happy," I responded. I felt an enticing warmth under my skin and couldn't help but smile even more.

The dad gently put her arm down and told her it wasn't nice to 'point at people.' He gave me an apologetic nod, but I couldn't stop smiling. The ride was so much more satisfying because of that.

I stood at the high street amidst many high-end restaurants when I stepped out of the second connecting bus. Rivers of people flowed on the pavement; Businessmen and women, shoppers, teenagers, tourists, civil servants. I went with the flow of the street looking at all the restaurants I was walking by. I went all the way to the end, where the chain of independent restaurants ended, and clothing shops began. I crossed the road and went back, to go in an Italian diner. I ordered a large pizza with Pepperoni and extra cheese.

Have you ever taken yourself out to a restaurant? If you have, you'll know that at first it is extremely weird. I felt watched and judged. Around me were families and friends, pockets of conversations, while I was in the middle, staring at the second plate in front of me with its accompanying shiny cutlery. I tried to indulge myself in the pizza, but I couldn't do it. I rushed and got the heck out of there.

I wasted some time by walking around aimlessly, until I reached the cinema. I pushed through the revolving door to see Roland leaning against a pillar.

"Kale? What the hell are you wearing?" He greeted me across the hall. "Did you feel like dusting off those *bad boys?*" He pointed down at my shoes.

"Shut up," I went in for our handshake. "I had a thing."

"A thing? You? Something I should know about?"

"Not really," I said.

"Alright, I will try to ignore this then. Let's get the popcorn and get in. The advertisements are already on, so we still have a couple minutes until the Forever movie starts. I hope it's good. I don't want to waste my money."

"Sweet or Salty?" a worker there asked me about my popcorn.

"Sweet," I said.

"I'll get the Salty, thank you." Roland leaned on the counter drooling at the huge pool of popcorn.

We paid and found our seats. We were a bit late, as the first few minutes of the movie was already playing. I was worried to disturb the other viewers, but luckily our seats were at a row that was not filled at all.

The movie was great! There was one scene in particular that struck me. The main character, a construction worker who finished his traineeship earlier in the movie, worked on a large project in Switzerland. After he clocked off for the shift he would teleport home to Australia, using the machine at the site. There he had a dream house with his wife and three kids. His wife was a volunteer charity worker based in South Africa who was growing famous. The kids were old enough to use the machine too and were going to a school in England.

The man worked hard, tirelessly, to help his family progress and live a comfortable life. The construction demanded long hours and his coworkers were looking down on him, given he was a newbie. On the day of his youngest son's birthday, he teleported to Denmark in order to buy him a watch, a present all of his kids got when they turned twelve. After the purchase he went to an alleyway to a teleporting machine. He dialled the coordinates, but ended up on a completely different world, seemingly all by himself, with nothing but the newly bought watch and his semi-empty lunchbox.

I loved the movie, but Roland was still torn, and couldn't decide if it warranted such hype from the media.

It started to darken after we left the cinema, so we decided to go home after a quick chat. He made me realise that I was a bit sunburnt, probably from the beach. When I made myself ready for bed, I saw what he was talking about. I had red blemishes on my face, and a red outline on my neck. Given I didn't see the waitress, I still felt like I had a brilliant day.

About that invitation to Trina and Roland's place, I decided to postpone it. I couldn't think of anything else than the exams that were getting closer quickly. They were disappointed, but they understood. To make it up to them, I invited them to Guine's café, after the last exam we all had.

"Those are so wonderful; don't you think Roland?" Trina said, caressing the bush leaves on the way to the entry gate.

"How did you find this place? I never even heard of it before," Roland asked me.

"I just stumbled upon it one day. I've come here quite often since then," I cracked open the squeaky gate to reveal a near to full patio, just like I found it the first time. Roland pointed out a free table near the edge, so naturally we took our seats. Around us were four to five tables of elderly people talking with each other. It sounded like some kind of club or society that had met up there. We put our backpacks down and waited for service.

"Really nice place," said Roland, looking all around.

"Wait till you see the inside. It really is wonderful. We can either wait here, or we can order inside. It's up to you really," I said.

"I'm too lazy right now," Trina said, sinking in her seat. "I don't care about what I get, I just need an energy *boost*. What are you always getting here?"

"I grew into cappuccino, so that. Oh, and I always take a brownie here. They have three kinds: white, dark, and milk chocolate. White is my favourite, so I'm going for that as well."

Roland sat up kindly, because the waitress was coming. "Welcome, what can I get for you?" I looked over to her and it was the waitress I was looking for before.

"I'll have a cappuccino and a white brownie please," I said.

"Oh, I know, I already have it written down. Nice to see you again," she smiled before giving her attention to Roland and Trina.

"I'll have the same please," Roland replied to her gesture.

"Make it three! But dark chocolate brownie for me," Trina said raising her hand up. To this point she was practically laying on her chair, with her feet far under the table.

"Awesome," the waitress whizzed off.

Until the coffee and brownies came, me and Roland were discussing how our exams went, while Trina was buried in her phone. We got stressed, because quite soon we realised that we had different answer lots of questions. That was one of the worst feelings ever. I really wanted Roland to do well, but the better he did, the worse I did. Where we found common ground then is to hope that we did badly enough for both of us to pass. That gave us a good giggle.

"The coffee and brownies for you," the waitress suddenly appeared next to me. Trina jumped up and sat properly. "I gave you two sugar packets on the side each, if it isn't enough inside you have more."

"Thank you," Trina pulled her brownie to herself. The waitress then went away in a good mood. Come to think of it, I never saw her not smiling.

"Enough of that gibber gabber about exams and all that. I thought we came here to forget about it. What I do want to know is what we will be wearing for the university ball."

"The suit I wore a thousand times already. It's black," I responded.

"I think you can only go in a black suit, but I'm not sure - Tie or bow tie?" Roland asked with urgency.

"I'll go with a tie. I'm thinking of just a classic look. Not too keen to look amazing, because 'what's the point?'"

"Okay. I like my tie to be recognizable, but you'll see me take it off most of the time. On the dancefloor I can't have my neck be strangled." He stirred his coffee. "I'll go all black. I like the classic look too."

Trina turned her head to me, wiping the last crumbles that survived off her mouth.

"Who are you going with?" Trina asked me.

"I don't know," I said. I really didn't want to hear that question.

"Come on man, hold your head up," Roland patted me on the shoulder. "Who do you have in mind?"

"No one. I think I will just go alone."

"To a ball? That is the only time you shouldn't come alone. I will kick you out personally if you do that," Trina raised her voice. "You must find someone. If not, we will!"

Trina was able to be quite intimidating sometimes. This was one of the times. She was a loving soul, but when she said that she would do something, she would do it no question.

"Okay, okay. Calm down," I saw some of the elderly people turn toward us.

We took a second to think, or at least I did.

"What about Ellie?" Roland asked me.

"She is taken. So are Sara and Stephanie," Trina added.

Me and Roland looked at each other puzzled.

"Who?" Roland took the fall.

"You know, Sara and Stephanie!" Trina said visibly annoyed.

"And you do this again. Can you remind me who they are instead of repeating their names for god's sake? You do this every time!" Roland rolled his eyes.

"Oh my god! Ellie, Sara, and Stephanie are always together. Sara is the one with the freckles and Stephanie is the tall one with too many bracelets on her arms."

"Okay, thanks a lot. But they are taken already. Do you have any other *candidates*?" Roland responded.

"I don't think so, the ball is just around the corner so most of them will be taken already," she said.

"What about you ask someone who isn't in our social group, or even doesn't study at all?"

"Roland, great idea, but one problem – I'm not the most social guy. Who the hell should I have met outside uni?"

"Work perhaps?" He looked at me all smug. Rightly so, he got me good, but there weren't any girls on my shifts anyways.

"Just ask one of the visitors on your next shift. You don't need butterflies in your stomach when you have them around you," Trina laughed.

"Very funny…"

"What about the waitress here?" Roland struck out of nowhere.

"I don't know," I said.

"Ah come on, you never know. It's so obvious she likes you. She is close to beaming next to you."

"She has to be kind to customers don't you know that?" I turned to find her among the crowd.

"That's partly true," the waitress said behind me. She scared me to the point where I nearly fell off my seat. "Easy there," she laughed. "Do you need anything else?"

It took a bit till I regained my composure, but Roland kept kicking me under the table, staring at me intently. "Yeah, I think Kale wanted something," he said.

That evil bastard. I loved him to bits, but at that moment I could strangle him without remorse. What a stunt to pull off...

"What can that be?" the waitress turned to me. It was tense, if you would be there, you would feel it too.

"Eh…" I struggled to get my words out.

"We were wondering whether you're studying at the university. I think I might have seen you," Roland smiled at me.

"Oh, I don't think it was me. I work here full-time for now, no time for studying."

"I see, because we will be attending a ball soon." I realised how it sounded just after I said it. I was nervous.

"Oh, that's nice for you guys. I hope you will have a grand time," she said.

Roland spoke up hastily, "What Kale here means is that he would like to invite you to the ball. What do you say?"

I saw Trina sipping her coffee knowing full well that the cup was empty. She was hiding her embarrassment. Too bad the waitress held my empty cup already in her hand.

The waitress turned red and was unsure of what to say. "You don't even know my name. Are you sure you don't want to invite another girl?"

"I don't want just another girl, that is why I'm asking you," I said.

I don't know where this came from, but I knew it was good by seeing Roland's thumbs up under the table.

"In that case I would happily accept!" She said.

"Awesome! Can I ask you for your number so we can stay in contact?" I saved the number in my phone, and she saw that I left out the 'name' section.

"It's Hanna," she said.

I felt a bit stupid to not have asked for her name in the beginning, but it was a relief that she helped me out.

"Thanks, Hanna. I'll text you," I said.

"Great!" her smile got bigger. I didn't know that it was possible. "Anything else?"

Trina finally broke her silence: "That's all, thanks."

For the rest of our meet up we talked about Hanna and that situation. Roland complimented me on the quick responses I gave, yet Trina thought my shyness and clumsy nature made the experience more wholesome and 'cute'. I would be lying if I said I wasn't euphoric. The last time I did something similar was when I asked a girl to prom. I asked two in fact, but both of them declined. From then on, I didn't dare to expose myself like that. If you're not next to people you can't be hurt, or at least I thought so then. Now I didn't recognise myself anymore.

I went home that day excited, not only because of Hanna, but also because tomorrow I would go to a poetry reading. I liked some poetry from time to time, and the university had welcomed a published poet that studied at the same university.

The reading was held in a quaint auditorium, distinct from all the others I have been to, because this one wasn't modernised yet. I hoped it would stay that way, as there was nothing more soulless than a sparkly clean, glass-bombarded symmetry, painted in white or silver.

I sat down in one of the front rows, with the auditorium being nearly filled to maximum capacity.

I expected the poet to be sitting at a long table, with perhaps other people, but no. She was sitting on a grand, purple armchair right on the edge of the elevated stage.

"What a fabulous armchair. I just wanted to let you know that it was the university who supplied me with this. I could never be as bold to carry such colour and *pazazz*." Her voice travelled with the help of her microphone clipped to her sweater.

She began telling her origin story briefly and gave subtle context to each of the poems she would recite. Some of them were electrifying, but others didn't really spark.

She continued with the next poem, one of the last of the meeting. It was called 'Aimlessly'.

"It is one of my older poems, having written it when I was a bit older than you." She looked at some professors: "Maybe not you", everyone chuckled. "The reason I wrote this poem in particular was because I didn't feel like I wasn't the master of myself. I still feel it sometimes, glimpses of what I somewhat believe to be the truth. I find myself in places that seem scripted, that seem directed by another player. When I wake from this illusion, I wonder whether this body is truly mine, or I'm just being pushed and pulled by invisible waves and tides around me."

Everyone was silent.

She then read it out loud:

Aimlessly

Don't you feel looped, enchained by something
Evil and divine? I sure feel it, that glittering lie,
That I see myself follow till the day I die.

Following crumbs like a hungry duckling. A
Soul directed by something that ensnares so
Many.

Lifeless bodies walking the pavements and
Drowned in crowds of their own kind. Slaves and
Shadows deprived by their own minds.

The promise of my own destiny slips through my fingers.
The pursuit of ecstasy was what splintered
My faith in me.

I got lost into her story and poem. I felt I knew what she was talking about, and for some odd reason, it was like she was talking directly to me. It made me hyper aware of where I was right now. In this auditorium, hidden in the corner of buildings too big to navigate by yourself without help. My head played my life back to all the situations that happened, or didn't happen, to lead me right here, sitting on this exact chair, listening to a poem by a person I never met before.

It was amazing, and when the meeting was wrapped up, I stood in line to get her autograph. There were many others who wanted one too. I saw her open the books to the first page and sign it with one vigorous hand motion, without a sign of difficulty. I could tell she did a lot of those in the past.

When it was my turn, I handed her the book opened on the page of the poem that struck me so much.

"You want an autograph here?" she looked at me.

"Yes, please." I held my hands together tightly.

"Alright."

After her autograph, she added a few words under it, that I could not read upside down.

She closed the book, and handed it to me, saying: "You're doing well."

I was confused, but I thanked her and walked out. Curious, what she wrote, I sat down on a ledge right outside the building.

'Aim Lesley' it said.

I didn't understand. I pondered what it could mean all the way home. When I tried to do some more research on the internet, I couldn't find her. But when I put in 'Lesley' with her surname, a news article popped up. It was about her husband, presumably boyfriend at the time she wrote the poem. He was a writer too, winning several prizes along the way. In one interview I watched, he was asked about his road to becoming a writer.

He said, "It was a treacherous ride. You know, it was one of those things that – that consumed you alive. You wonder whether it will spit you out, or take your life."

"*How* did you achieve this success? What was the secret?" The interviewer said.

"My wife. She was always there. Before all this fame, years ago when I didn't know what the hell I was doing, she kept me in shape. She saw me slip up time and time again, with alcohol and drugs, but she never left me."

"How did it feel then? What was the problem do you think?"

"I didn't know what I was doing. I just did what everybody else wanted me to do, but she taught me otherwise."

Chapter Six

A nthony asked me to help him guide tour groups around our section. Because our zoo was opening a large sea aquarium, there had been record-breaking amounts of bookings. It took them three and a half years to finish that, but *finally* we had it. Anthony and I had to stop to use it as a standing joke.

For three days straight I had planned to work ten-hour shifts in order to help as much as I could.

Arriving at work on the first day, I was motivated and excited to see Anthony. He was too, because first thing I stepped into the room he dropped everything he was doing and came to me.

"That is what we were waiting for! Great to see you!" He gave me, what I thought was the first hug ever. He didn't go easy either. He crushed me and my bag without breaking a sweat.

"Mhm," I gasped for air.

Upon his release I dropped my bag and took a couple of deep breaths.

"I knew you were strong, but *wow*," I began to laugh.

"Ah it's nothing, you'll be the same when you have to wrestle with your little boys every night," he said going to the fridge. "Here you go, I got some reserves for those three days."

I saw a red bottle flying towards me right in time. It hit my chest, but my flailing arms somehow caught it awkwardly.

"Thanks Anthony… Strawberry and… Banana?"

"Of course, I bought others too, but I remember you telling me that this flavour was for your happy days, and no doubt we will be having a great time!" He slammed the fridge close and clasped his hands loudly. "So, let's get cracking, shall we?"

"Hang on, I just came in. I need to change first."

"Fine." He looked like a kid that wasn't allowed a cookie.

"But you know, while I get ready we can go over the plan and so forth. I want to know what will happen during my first full-time shifts," I said.

"Alright! So, listen up. First, we…"

The day was all planned out. We both wrote down our timetables for the day, so we could coordinate our breaks. From a dusty box in the garage, we took out walkie-talkies that we never used before, and clipped them each on our belts. It took some time to figure out how they worked.

Most of the time we would tour a group at the same time, but we took opposing routes so we wouldn't clash. To check whether we were going at a good pace, we would use two trees that stood right across each other as checkpoints.

A couple groups in, I was leading a class of high schoolers. We just reached the checkpoint tree.

"Let's pause here for a little bit," I said.

"Wow, that tree didn't look that big from afar," the teacher looked up in awe.

"Yeah, many underestimate the height of this dome. As I've said before the tallest point is fourteen and a half metres above the ground. Given the standards of trees not impressive at all, but it seems so big as everything around it is so small, with all those bushes and flowers."

The teenagers were more interested than I thought. Of course, some were just there because they had to, giggling and joking around all the time.

"What class do you teach, if you don't mind me asking?" I asked the teacher.

"Oh, I'm just a math teacher. I don't know a lot about *biological thingies*," she laughed.

"That's awesome," I said. "When I see groups such as these, they take me back a couple years. I hold these memories dear. Maths too, I'll have you know, I was quite good at it. Now though, I don't have a lot of equations to solve."

"Oh! Lovely to hear that!" The students around her either rolled their eyes or were focused on every word I said.

"Are you a university student, or do you *just* work here?" A girl next to me asked.

"I'm a student actually, why?"

"How do you like it? We are on our penultimate year and everyone is wondering what they should do after," she said.

"W-Well, if you already found a field you're interested in, I think university helps you get closer to that. However, if you didn't find anything particular yet, keep looking. At least –"

My walkie talkie went off. Anthony and his group reached the other tree.

"– At least you know what you don't like. That's a start."

The girl looked satisfied with that answer, so was the teacher, that looked rather proud. I wasn't sure whether it was about me liking maths, or about the corny speech about university I just gave, but she gave me one of the nods of approval. You know, the nod you get from a superior as soon as you have proven yourself worthy. Felt good to be honest.

We quickly gathered the group back together and continued following the paths towards the ending section.

"And here usually you can see a butterfly called 'The red Admiral.' They are a common species in our region. They are easily to spot, as they have black wings with white spots on their tips and a red or orange line going through it – Oh like here for instance, we can see three of them together." I pointed towards a dense bush of flowers.

While continuing to inform the group, Anthony showed up and began listening to every word I said. His group finished the tour. Nobody saw him, as he lurked in the back crossing his arms in judgement.

I gave him a mean look for a split of a second, while he stuck his tongue out.

"When we continue now, on the right you can see one of the best butterfly bushes around; the 'Buddleia Davidii'. Easily distinguishable by its purple nature. Look at how many butterflies fly around it!" I pointed.

Anthony kept testing my patience, so I decided to rat him out by saying, "Oh, and here is my teacher and coworker Anthony! How are you doing?"

The group turned around to see a surprised Anthony standing awkwardly.

"Hi, there folks. You know, as his boss I have to make sure all he says is true, and so far he is doing pretty well."

The group was smiling and laughing a bit.

"Anthony will leave us now, as his break just began, so let's move on towards the other side where we will see another haven for the beauties; the coneflower patch."

I opened the office door, when I finished the tour, to see Anthony clapping.

"Well played sir, well played," he said.

"Thank you very much."

"Didn't know you'd have the guts to set me up like this, but here we are. A bold move I'll give you that."

"I'm learning from the best." I gave him a high five.

"Let's plan the next day a bit, so we can go home as soon as the last group is dealt with," Anthony said.

The plan was to come early the next day to scan the dome for any last-minute touch ups. We would do a general sweep of checking the bins and benches as well, cleaning where necessary. We had fourteen groups that day, which we would get done one by one like that day - in sync.

The second day went as planned, smooth but became quite tedious. I did make a couple mistakes where I had to correct myself, and one time I couldn't answer a man's question. That was embarrassing, but I used the fact that I was still learning as an excuse. Anthony taught me to do that in case things got 'rowdy' as he would say. Luckily, we didn't have any nightmare visitors that pluck flowers, throw soil around, or grab butterflies to name a few. Yes, these happened already.

Anyhow, talking of nightmares, my third and final day of my longer shifts began tragically. I poured myself a bowl of cereal for breakfast, just to realise I was out of milk. That's where I've learned that mixing it with water wasn't too good of an idea. Having finished that travesty, I ate a banana to shift the taste to something different, but my mood was shot from then on... The feeling of upcoming doom when you mess up breakfast.

When I arrived in the office, I couldn't see Anthony around. I made myself at home and opened the fridge to see the remainder of the three-day reserves. I took a piece of cake, leaving the last slice for Anthony and began munching it.

"Beware, the species is easy to startle. We see him in its natural environment – the fridge. Every day it seeks out food, that beyond his comprehension just appears inside that mysterious box," Anthony said silently, holding a brush as a microphone.

I looked at him with crumbs on my cheek.

"Oh no!" He jumped "It has seen us. Get back!"

"Me'er shay," I mumbled with a fool mouth.

"It can talk, but we can't understand what it's saying."

I wiped my face with my sleeve and swallowed the huge chunk of cake.

"Never change," I smirked. "How are you doing?"

"I should ask you." He gave up his gimmick. "You're a tad early. You've been motivated recently."

"Yeah, well, what can I say? When someone is lucky enough to be working with you… it's the Anthony effect."

He laughed out loud.

"Anthony effect ha?" He swiped his imaginary dust off his shoulder. "Well then, good on me."

I took my shoes off and began putting on the heavy work boots.

"I've inspected our gear, you know? I've been wearing the same shoes for ages now. I don't have to mention the uniforms, mine has its colour so faded it's becoming transparent."

He wasn't wrong. The boots that he already had on were covered in scratches and bruises. The rubber sole was completely wore out. The uniforms we got were brown, but his had become a sort of light orangy colour.

Anthony raised a closed fist and began commanding with his left arm behind him: "It's time my dear peasant, for the rough days behind us have forced us to change. As leader peasant of the office, I mustered the courage to communicate our despair to the king! They have answered!"

His left arm stretched outwards revealing two T-shirts on a hanger dangling on his index finger.

"Black or Grey?" He asked in a high-pitched tone.

I stood up with one shoe on, glaring at the T-shirts as if they were relics.

"As just a lowly peasant, my humble, non-significant opinion is… Black," I said.

"What?" Anthony broke character again and let his arms drop. "Why?"

"Why not?"

"I was confident you'd say Grey. I love that colour. Maybe the pants will change your mind?"

I followed him to the garage, still with one damn shoe on, where two middle-sized boxes stood unevenly on the ground. Inside I could go through the uniforms: T-shirts, pants, socks, jumpers, and rain jackets.

"I don't know," I said, rustling and squeezing the fabric in my hands. "I think I still prefer the black colour".

"How should we decide then. We have to work in the same-coloured uniform, I think that goes without saying."

I threw the jumper I was holding into the box and smashed a closed fist against my open palm.

"Best of three," I said.

"Alright then, may the proudest peasant win."

"You have no chance old man."

We started work all in grey. While I was inspecting the place before the groups came, I could immediately tell grey was a horrific choice. The sweat was immediately noticeable. No problem for Anthony however, because he never sweated.

The inspection went smoothly, with just a couple things to iron out and we were good to go.

Just before my first group, I decided to put on a fresh T-shirt and a jumper on top. When I left the office, I saw a few smaller groups standing in at the dome entrance. This wasn't a group reservation but an open tour. I liked those more, as they tended to behave better. It was probably because they didn't want to embarrass themselves in front of strangers.

"Hello everyone! You are here for the first tour of the day am I right?" I scanned through the group quickly to see who would be brave enough to answer me.

"Yes, I believe so." An older man with a magnificent beard and a cane was the chosen one. "The one at 8:30".

"Thank you, sir," I nodded at him. I quickly counted the heads of everyone in front of me. "As some could be late, we will wait a few more minutes. While we wait, feel free to take the various leaflets on this stand informing you about the dome structure, the butterflies, and more."

Usually, one person of each small group of family or friends would go to take the leaflets. It was so funny sometimes to see how they'd behave. One time a mother of three came to pick the leaflets. She stood there for a solid fifteen seconds debating which one to choose. Her face was comical when I told her all of them were the same, but the different colour signified a different language. I laughed on the inside while she scurried back to her family.

"Sir," the bearded man with the cane interrupted my thoughts, "May I ask how long the tour will last?"

"It lasts for over an hour, but usually no longer than an hour and ten minutes. Do you need to be somewhere after the tour?"

"No, it's not that," a woman of comparable age next to him said to me. "It's just that we are not the youngest *sprouts* anymore, and we could use a break or two if that is alright with you."

"Oh, that is no problem at all. Thank you for coming up to me. There are a couple places with benches on our path, and I will make sure to keep the breaks in mind." I then turned to the path in front of us and pointed towards various points on the path. "We will take our first break over there, can you see it?"

"Ah yes," the elderly man said. "I would appreciate it if you could tell me about the next points throughout the path. It will make it easier to manage my efforts," he chuckled.

"Will do sir," I smiled. I turned back towards the others and counted the people again. I found the group had grown by a couple more people. With that we started the tour, albeit two minutes late.

I was pleased to have the frequent brakes, because I could feel sweat drops trickle down my back. My forearms were gleaming in the bright dome, all slippery when my hand ran through it.

By midway I could hear someone from the group say, "I didn't know you had moths too."

I tried to find the person who said that, but they were way in the back of the group.

"We don't," I said.

The visitors stepped aside to reveal Hanna.

"Then what is that?" she said.

"Ehm- Let me see," I skipped to her. I began sweating even more if that was possible. My mind raced and as soon as I saw what she was on about I cleared my throat.

"It's a Chequered Skipper. It- it looks kind of like a moth, but in fact is one of our rarer species. Good find."

Before she could answer back, I already turned away and lead the group further. "And now what we will try to find is…"

She didn't say anything else, until the tour ended. When all the group members dispersed, I could see her gunning straight toward me. I tried to *seem* to be busy, even though I was. I grabbed a leaflet quickly and opened it.

"Checking up on something?" She said.

"Oh! Hi! Yes, need to look up a detail I wasn't sure of."

It was still weird to see her in personal clothes, just like the time at the church. It used to be her black uniform from neck to toe. However, it was the first time I saw her be completely calm, without the rush of having to go to customers or running after her grandparents.

"One detail you might've skipped is that it's upside down." She grabbed a leaflet and tried to read it upside down.

"What?" Then I clocked that she was right.

"If you can read it like this then I'm mightily impressed." I closed the leaflet in embarrassment.

"The moth thing was a good question," I said. "I don't know what people think most of the time *if* they have the chance to see it. It does look like one."

"It flew towards me. *I* am the chosen one," she said jokingly. "Anyway, nice to see you work for a change. Is this what you do all the time?"

"Partly. Me and my colleague have to make sure everything is in tip top shape. That includes looking out for the plants, controlling the humidity and temperature in the dome, spraying for diseases etcetera, etcetera."

"And what about the breeding you looked at last time? That was the main reason I came." I saw Anthony behind her wanting to speak to me, but waving his hand at me, thinking he could say it later. "I didn't know you worked here, but I had a sneaky suspicion."

We both laughed.

"Well, we do breed a couple species. It's not that simple as you think."

"Can I see?" she was all ready to go.

"I'm sorry, breeding is strictly for staff. I would show you more things, but we are on a tight schedule. The next group is here in roughly five minutes," I said.

I could see her smile shrink. "That is a shame. I don't want to be a bother to you, so I will let you do your work. Come to think of it, you never interrupted my work."

"I'm sorry, you just picked the busiest weekend we had for a long while."

"Why is that?"

"Haven't you heard about the new aquarium they opened up? You should check it out, it's amazing!" I said. I never thought I would recommend another part of the zoo, as me and Anthony were childishly proud of our own work.

"Alright, I can check it out. I'm in the zoo already, so why not? But I bet it won't be nothing compared to your butterfly dome, it's gorgeous."

That was the best complement I have ever received from a girl. I blushed hard.

She took a couple steps back to signify that she was leaving, raising her hand for a small wave.

"Bye now, thanks for the tour," she said. "Oh, and by the way, you might want to get changed, your sweater is getting wet."

Ouch.

After that intense weekend I could come to work on Monday later than usual. Now as a full-time worker I could choose my hours, and for the beginning I chose to do some overtime to save up some money.

With the exams finished though, Trina convinced me to be looser, and let myself relax. Trina told me about a party her and Roland were doing at their place and that they would love me to come, just like last time. I told her I had work, but Trina insisted, telling me that I wouldn't regret it. Something about her cheeky smile made me uneasy.

During work I had Trina's mission in mind, but Anthony wasn't to be seen in the office when I walked in. A quick scan of our dome told me that he wasn't there either. I just did the usual; put on the still dry grey outfit and went out to hunt down plant diseases. At that point you could have called me the pathogen hunter, which I thought sounded medieval and badass. Anyway, that was what I did.

I did nearly the full sweep until I finally saw Anthony.

"Anthony!" I shouted happily.

"Kale!" he matched the energy.

"I was worried they fired you for a second there!" I took off my dirt covered gloves. "How are you doing?"

"They would never fire me," we laughed. "I had to attend a meeting concerning the three hard workdays we put in. I forgot about it, so I didn't give you any notice. I'm sorry for that." He looked around to see what a good job I had done. "We analysed how everything went and any corrections we could make. I'm happy to say that we did very well, only second to the new aquarium, which would be obviously first. I am meant to congratulate you from the managers."

He saw my relief in my face.

"Awesome," I said. "That's good to hear. What about the corrections?"

"There are a few things, but nothing major. I will tell you later on, or tomorrow. I see you managed amazingly by yourself. Thanks for doing diligent work without me around. I will be in the office, meet me there for your well-earned break."

145

I did just that, finished up the last inspections, and after a particularly sick bush removal, I joined him in the office.

"I'm very proud of you," he said when I opened the fridge. "You are doing great!"

I smiled behind the open fridge door.

"Do you want anything?" I asked him.

"No, thank you." I closed the door and sat down. "I meant to ask; how did your exams go?"

"They went alright. Not sure if brilliantly, but I passed for sure, I think." I gulped down a bottle of juice. "I am glad it's over."

"I'm sure you are. What are your plans now? Do you celebrate somehow, or you just move on with what you do?"

"I'm not sure yet. Like, I was invited to one party, but I got work, so there's that."

"When is that?" Anthony flipped open his calendar, dropping whatever he was doing. "What date?"

"It's in three days... Here" I pointed at the calendar.

"Alright, *son*." He crossed my work shift then, as well as the next day. "You got my pass. You don't have to come the next day either. For that, you'll come and help me with the physical inventory next Tuesday, if that's alright with you."

I was indeed alright with it. No, even better, I was ecstatic.

"You deserve it *son*. I'll let you enjoy your break now. I still have some forms to fill."

Trina and Roland loved Anthony when I told them about what he did. For some reason, Trina couldn't contain herself and actually called me, in order to tell me how happy she was. Out of the ordinary for sure, but wholesome.

Skipping two days ahead, I saw myself walking on the familiar street, which welcomed me with faint bass when I turned the corner. I saw groups of people on curbs, taxi's pulling up, I heard laughing and music. Many of the faces were familiar, but there were still many that I haven't seen yet. Among them I saw Roland. I called out his name.

"Oh Kale." He excused himself from the group he was talking to. "I'm so happy you could make it." I was ready for the handshake, but he went in for a hug.

"Do you know all those people? Also, is it okay with the neighbours?"

"Oh of course it is! I let them know. It is the last party we will do this summer. We have plans to move out. Also! We finished our exams, so it's time to party!"

I hoped he would answer my first question too, but I trusted him to know what he was doing. Besides, it was their house, their party, so who was I to question that.

The party looked very similar to the one that I went to last time. The same music and the same perfumes floating around in the rooms. Cups and bottles still filled the tables, making me wonder if they actually tidied up after the last one. However, this time I could see more snacks and cake.

"Make yourself comfortable. You can put your stuff in my room as always. Also, I heard from Trina that you were looking for more food last time, so I made everyone take something with them for the party."

"Oh, why didn't you tell me to bring something for the party? I just took something for myself," I said.

"I want you to feel good. Don't worry, please. And don't you dare head off and get something from the corner shop while I'm not looking."

He knew me too well.

"I got loads of juices and snacks with me, that I think will last me for the whole night. If you need something, just go to your room and take it out my bag," I said.

"Sure thing, thanks so much," he said. "Now go and party, I will see you around. Trina is in there somewhere; she is waiting for you to come."

So, in I went and put my things in his room. I checked the bag to make sure no bottles were leaking. While I did that, the door opened. It was Trina.

"Hello there." She hugged me too, squeezing me from behind.

"Why is everyone so happy?" I said.

"Well, I guess we are excited for today. We finished our exams! Maybe you should ask yourself why you aren't happy?"

"I am happy," I said.

"And yet I can't see a smile."

I was smiling at her though. I wasn't sure what she meant by that.

"I am smiling," I let my thoughts speak out.

"You are, but not really. I bet it will change tonight though, you'll see!"

I doubted her big time.

"What have you been up to lately, outside of working and taking my boyfriend to the movies," she laughed. "I wished he would do that to me more often to be honest. But you know… a girl could only wish."

"Does he know that you want to go to the cinema? Did you ask?"

"Well, no! But he should know I love movies and put one and two together!"

"Well then, you'll just be miserable, and he wouldn't know why."

She looked at me funny. "Since when did you become the relationship expert? I will see for myself I guess." She giggled for some odd reason.

We then began talking about some random stuff, as you do at a party. We went on and on, already sitting on Roland's bed, until another guy just popped in holding his jacket.

He froze "Ehmm- Eh," and he closed the door again.

Trina stood up and opened the door again.

"It's fine, we're just friends. Nothing's happening, just having a deep talk," she said.

We didn't actually, but I wasn't there to be ruining our escape of awkwardness. The guy just threw his jacket onto the table, without stepping into the room.

"Then I won't intrude," he said, walking off into the loud abyss.

"We should be joining them anyway," Trina said, still holding the door open. "We are here for the party and not for a one-on-one session!"

She was right. I gathered my juice supplies and joined her out. Trina made me promise that I'd dance with her that same evening, but only after 'we got grooving'. Again, I didn't really know what she meant, but I just nodded, and to my surprise I looked forward to the party, more than I thought anyway.

I hovered from one place to another, talking to groups of people I knew, and got forced to talk with those that I didn't. Nice people with a wide variety of humour. I had to be careful not to mix up a joke that I'd normally say to one group, and say it to another that had different humour. Of course, that happened, and I had to excuse myself to the bathroom to quickly reflect what my life had come to.

After loitering about for long enough, I heard a familiar voice, that didn't belong to Roland, Trina, or anybody I met before at the party.

"I'm sorry I am late, but I had to do over hours as we were short on staff," she said.

I couldn't see her with people in the way, but I could see Roland's huge smile on his face, replying to her. When I shifted to the side, I saw Hanna.

"Hanna," I appeared at her side.

"Kale!" she hugged me tightly. "Another person I know at the party! That makes three," she put up three fingers.

"Good to see you! I'll head off, if you need me just find me and I'm happy to help," Roland said, shifting his weight already away from Hanna.

"Where are you going?" She was puzzled.

Roland took a brief second to figure out his response. "I-I need to look around if everyone is okay. You know, I'm the host, so it's my responsibility. I'll catch you later for sure."

As he quickly scurried off, he left me alone with Hanna.

"Fun place," she said.

"Don't you want to leave your jacket behind? It's very stuffy in here with all those people."

"Maybe a bit later, thanks. I want to look around this place. Do you know everyone in here Kale?"

"Not nearly as many as I probably should. I know a couple though."

"Ahh, I see. I know this is kind of rude at first, but can I get something to drink? I didn't have enough time to buy anything for myself, and I had water all day. I need something different."

"I'm sure Roland wouldn't mind you taking anything you need from the cupboards, as long as it's discreet, otherwise everyone will do it, and I will get the brunt of his funny rage. Other than that, you can steal from someone else, or from me."

"Alright. What do you have?" She crossed her arms in drama and over-acted curiosity.

"Well, I am not much of a drinker, so I have loads of juice and snacks if you want."

"What flavours?"

"Let me see… I have Banana and Strawberry, just Strawberry, Orange, Apple, and, last but not least, Multifruit."

Her surprised expression made me laugh, as my voice began shaking for a reason unbeknownst to me. A tightness in my gut took away my focus on my speech, or her.

"Are you okay?" She tapped my forearm.

"Yes, why?"

"I'd just asked you a question, but I assume you've spaced out."

Damn, it really did happen again.

"Don't worry, it's fine. I'm slowly getting used to it. It's quite adorable to be honest. Anyways –" she said.

Does she expect me to just roll over what she just said? Not sure, but it made my face burn up and the gut tightness had gotten worse. I caught myself 'spacing out' again, so I listened to the rest of what she had to say.

"- so, let's go?"

I nodded.

I stood there waiting for her to move, so I could follow, but she waited for me.

"So?" A bit frustrated she asked me anew.

I had no clue how to get out of this one. She was eating me up alive and there was nothing I could do.

"Hanna! Nice to see you!" Trina, my saviour, came for the rescue. "I'm so glad you could make it! I was worried you wouldn't come, or that you got lost."

"No, just work things. When I got your invitation, I was so surprised. At first, I had to really scramble my brain to know who you were, but in the end, I got it. You should've just said Kale's name," they both laughed.

"Let me take your things and show you around. I presume Kale didn't do it yet." Trina abducted Hanna. "Did you meet Roland yet? He is somewhere around here- "

They went upstairs.

I thanked Trina profusely the day after for saving me then.

I was sitting with some new people I met. We came together when one of them asked if anyone wanted to play cards. I had nothing better to do, so I accepted. We cleared the table of the booze and wiped all the stickiness off it. Nothing worse than a table that stuck to your skin when you leaned on it.

We discussed the house rules and quickly began playing. Our table was in a corner, and me being me, I took the seat right at the edge. I always like to sit in confined spaces where there was nothing behind me. It made me feel at ease, and didn't require me to look behind me every now and again. The number of times I got a neck strain from that…

We were in our own bubble and during the game we got to know each other more. The two undergrads were Tyler and Rianne. The postgraduate was half Japanese and half English, by the name of Takara.

I liked to be competitive, but the game that we played was a French twist, introduced by Rianne. I wasn't able to remember the name of it exactly, but it was pretty difficult to learn. Till the end, when we decided to stop playing, I didn't figure out all the rules. There was too much counting involved.

Anyway, I had a blast and I felt I could finally connect interests with someone.

I went out to get some fresh air, as the inside of the windows were fogged up and everyone's breath lingered in the rooms.

Roland's house included a garden, where he had a terrace. I leaned against one of its thin wooden pillars and just let my thoughts float away. It wasn't long until Hanna came by and leaned against the same pillar on the opposite side.

"I'm suffocating in there too. I forgot how exhausting parties can be at times," she said.

"Yes, that's true. Do you want juice? I was just about to go in to get some anyway."

That was a lie.

"If you wouldn't mind. I'd love some," she sat down, still leaning against the pillar.

I went back to Roland's room, weaving around couples. I grabbed the whole bag, as I realised, I forgot to ask what she wanted specifically. I dropped the bag beside Hanna and sat down the same way she did on the other side of the pillar.

"Thank you so much! Can I take any, or do you have your favourite juice I shouldn't touch?" She giggled, reaching down the bag inspecting my taste.

"Take whatever."

I saw her take the Banana and Strawberry taste. That was my favourite, and I wanted it so badly. I had to do with plain old orange juice then.

"Cheers!" I said, opening the plastic bottle.

"Cheers! To new experiences!"

"Looking forward to the ball?" I asked, trying to make conversation.

"Oh, yes. You see, it's my first ball ever."

"What about prom?" I asked.

"Well – it's a long story, but I ended up not going. But I am excited for this one! A bit scared but excited. You?"

"I didn't have loads to think about really, because I didn't think I'd go to be honest. But now that I am, I think I'm scared too," I said.

I heard the popping of the bottle and scratching. I took a glance to what she was doing.

"I like to scrape off the piece of paper on the bottles," she explained herself.

I took out a creampuff that I wrapped with aluminium foil out of the bag. When I opened it up, I was astonished to see it wasn't ruined nearly as much as I thought.

"You are a sweet tooth, aren't you? All the brownies, the creampuffs, the other day at the church." She was the one who peeked over her shoulder this time.

I had my mouth full already, so I just nodded and smiled.

"Just thinking of that day, the church thing I mean," she continued. "It was so funny. My grandparents asked me later how I knew 'that guy', and my grandmother called you weird, carrying so many bakery paper bags and eating at the entrance of the church. Very specific."

"But it was raining!" I defended myself once I swallowed half the creampuff that I had just attacked.

"I wonder, did you go in?" She followed up.

"What, the church?"

"Yes, when I left, I still saw you at the entrance."

"Yes, I did," I told her.

"So… what do you think? Beautiful, isn't it?"

She was so hyped up to talk about it, so I just followed along.

"Yeah, it was alright. A bit spooky, the priest greeted me just when I left," I said.

Hanna looked confused. She thought about what I have said intently, so much so her eyebrows dropped down aggressively.

"It can't be, the priest left half way through our meeting as he had to go teach kids for their communion. We all left, leaving the church open for the priest to come back and close it."

"No, no. He was still there. I remember it exactly," I said.

"But it is impossible. There was no one left." She began to raise her voice a tad. "Ok, what does he look like?"

"He stood right under the huge hanging cross as I was at the door, so it was far away. Obviously, he had his priest clothes on, that's how I knew he was a priest in the first place. His hair was short and grey."

"Firstly, it's called a 'cassock' – the priest clothes. Secondly, our priest is bald."

She made me think twice of what I saw, and I began doubting myself. It was a brief moment anyway, so I could have messed up. I conceded and her tone returned back to normal.

Trying to avoid silence after this moment, I asked her: "Do you like going to the church?"

"Well, yes! What about you? Do you believe in something out there?" She took a snack from my bag.

"I did once, but I lost it. I did go to church with my mum, but ever since my parents got divorced, I didn't bother anymore."

"Oh no, I'm sorry to hear that. So, you went just to make your mum happy?"

"Not entirely. Like, it was a big part don't get me wrong, but I did believe that there was something that holds it together. I believed in a just and fair world, but that didn't work out well."

"I see. Life can be disappointing, for sure. I had my fair share too. I would've loved to go to church with my mother, but I was raised in an atheist household. Luckily my grandparents introduced me to it two years ago, and I hold it dear ever since." She took out a necklace with an angel on it, which hid underneath her T-shirt. "I am never really alone, and this reminds me of that fact."

I didn't know what to say. I didn't want to destroy her optimism and joy. I just smiled and drank my juice.

155

"I'm just curious what is out there. Really curious," she continued.

"Yes, I mean it is interesting, but it does scare me," I acknowledged.

"How so?"

"Well, if it something out there does exist, what about the mistakes we make here; won't they hurt us over there? And what if it's completely different to how we think? Maybe the rules we live by are completely wrong."

"Yeah, I get your point."

"I'm sorry to be that negative," I stepped down my scepticism.

"No, it's alright. I mean, you're right. How can we know? If we *did* know about it, there would be only one religion, right? That's why we call ourselves 'believers' and not 'knowers'. And about the world that comes after, if there is one in the first place, it will surely be different to what we expect. It goes beyond our earthly experiences, so naturally, it will be something completely new. We can have some thoughts or expectations that it might meet, but the overall experience will be absolutely unique. It's like reading a book and imagining all the scenes in your head. Then you see the movie adaptation and with it the director's imagination. They are similar, but completely different at the same time."

"And what about the mistakes we make?" I asked.

"Well, what I think, is that mistakes don't matter at all. You can make all the mistakes in the world, that doesn't make you bad. What does matter is your intention. Life doesn't require us to become the best, but only that we try our best."

It was then when the conversation gripped me. We continued talking about religion, which then morphed into other subjects.

"Aw damn, we have no more snacks left." I looked into the bag, seeing only a bunch of empty wrappers and bottles. At the bottom I could feel 2 juices that weren't touched yet.

"Do you want to head inside maybe?" She stood up from the hard floor.

"Yeah, I'll throw the things into the bin. You go ahead."

I lost her as soon as she entered the packed house. I went to the pavement and threw all the trash into the garbage container.

I put my backpack into my room and returned to the lively party. I saw Hanna with Trina and her friends. It seemed Hanna was having a fun time, so I didn't want to interrupt that. I saw Rianne too, playing beer pong with others.

A stranger caught me and gave out a grand monologue. He didn't want to stop talking.

"Sorry, I would like to continue our talk, but I need to go to the bathroom," I said to him.

I went upstairs, sat down on the stairs for a couple minutes and went back down to join Rianne. I did feel bad for the guy, but I couldn't be patient for any longer.

"Hi again, can I join you?" I said to her.

"Oh, ye-yes," she said. Rianne didn't look at me, but kept staring at my shoulder when she was talking to me. "Do I know you? You seem – like I know you."

She rocked from side to side trying to throw the ping pong ball into the cups on the other side of a table. She did pretty well considering her 'state'.

"You try one *mate*," a guy at the other side of the table said. He threw me a ball. "But if you try, you will have to drink when I hit one."

I threw it and hit the rim; it bounced off to the right hitting a girl in the face.

"Bullseye!" The same guy said.

The girl I hit by mistake held her cheek and laughed it off.

"Sorry!" I shouted across to her. I didn't think she heard me.

Like it always happens, this guy, without thinking too much about it, threw the ball into one of my cups.

"Drink up now *mate*," he said.

"Seems like a con," I said. "I should've never accepted your deal."

Then I understood why Rianne was so... limp.

I drank the cup and handed him the ball, squinting my eyes hard trying to get it all down.

"Have fun," I said, fully knowing that Rianne would lose the game horribly.

"You give up?" Rianne shouted. "I didn't think you'd do that. *I* will fight for you!" She then punched her chest twice.

She wasn't the only one who was standing on their last legs. Actually, me and Hanna were the two most sober people there. But after looking around, I couldn't find her.

"She probably left," I said to myself.

Slowly but surely the groups dispersed and when the majority had left, I wanted to go too, but I saw Trina clearing the tables all by herself. I left my bag leaning against the wall and began throwing the whole mess into rubbish bins.

"Oh, thank you Kale! I would never ask, but I am happy for your help."

I felt bad for her, as from her surprise I could tell that not many people help her clean most of the time. People just arrive, have a fun time in her expense, and leave without a second thought. It did hurt.

The rubbish was quickly taken care off because I could just slide everything off the edge of the tables with my forearm. Trina gave me a wet towel to wipe the surfaces.

"It doesn't have to be too thorough. I know you're tired. I just want to have something done already, so I don't wake up tomorrow stuck in this hell hole," she said.

I just nodded.

While I was wiping the last table I saw, Trina stood at the other end with her arms crossed.

"You promised me we would dance!" Trina said frustratingly.

I just looked at her, embarrassed above all else.

"But I can't be mad at you, you did exactly what we had hoped. I wouldn't say I watched you, as that would be creepy, but I did look out for you occasionally to see how you were doing," she added.

"Well, thanks for that, but I don't know what else to do. Like, it was nice and all, but what now?"

Trina sighed. "Ok, if I have to spell it out for you, then fine. She gave you her *number* for a reason. Remember? Don't call, make sure you text, and I beg you, don't text her today. I would say give it two or three days."

"Alright."

Trina punched me on my shoulder and stretched out her pinkie.

"Not alright," she said. "You have to swear. We didn't do all this for you to mess it up. We believe in you!"

But I didn't ask them to do anything. I really did appreciate their help, but it made me feel guilty to some degree.

After that promise I took my stuff and headed home, exhausted.

It took me two days to text her; I was sitting in the office, bored out of my mind. I thought I would use my time to figure out what to write. She responded nearly instantly. We wrote back and forth until we agreed to meet the next day after my final lecture.

The next day I jumped out of bed in full excitement. There weren't a lot of occasions where I could use my expensive hair gel, but just like at the cinema with Roland, I styled it well. I entered the lecture hall earlier than usual. So early in fact, that I had to reserve a seat for Roland.

"You are meeting up with Hanna, aren't you?" Roland stood on the stairs next to my row of seats with his hands in his pockets.

"Good morning to you too," I smiled. "And yes, you're exactly right."

"Ding, ding, ding! You've guessed correctly! You win one million pounds!" He raised his hands. "Congratulations to the winner!" He bowed down while I clapped laughing. Other students who were there either joined in or hated Roland for being so loud during a morning. "So, what's up, what are you going to do?" He sat down.

"She's going to wait for me outside, and then we're going to the park. I'm hungry, so we will probably ask to grab a bite at the burger stand."

"I'm happy for you man. I thought you wouldn't have the balls to text her. But when Trina told me that you promised, I knew you'd do it. Afterall, if you wouldn't promise, it would be your *kinda* thing to disappear to another country for that."

"Now that you give me the idea…" We laughed.

The lecture started soon after and to be honest, I didn't listen to one single word the professor said. She gave us a whole summary of what we have learned, and how the courses next semester would look like.

It felt like years till she closed that lecture, "Thank you for coming to this voluntary lecture. I hope your exams went well and I will see you after the summer."

I jumped up first while everyone was packing up their stuff. I took a step to the stairs, but Roland pulled me back by my backpack.

"Roland?"

"Wait for two minutes. You cannot be the first out of here. What do you think it will look like from her point of view? You need to stay cool."

"Right. Thanks for that."

"We will go out together, just hold on. I will go to the toilet, and then we will go."

Most people left already when we went out. As soon as we left the building, we scanned for her, but nobody was waiting.

"She will come, don't worry. I will leave you here."

"Why?"

"Kale, if she sees us together waiting for her, she knows that you told me all about the meet up. Keep it to yourself for now. Good luck."

I didn't know a lot about all these things, but that made sense. We did our awesome handshake, and he made his way home. I didn't feel like standing, so I sat down on a short ledge. Campus became eerily quiet. Those who wandered around were either home or in class. It wasn't as sunny of a day for people to chill. The ledge was made up of old stone, which squashed my hamstrings. My phone, that I held on tightly, didn't give me any hope. Every few seconds, I could feel something inside me just pass away. I should've known that something was wrong when fifteen minutes passed with no sign of her or any receiving messages.

"Not again," I said thinking about the situation with Ben.

I slid off the ledge, put on my backpack, and began my way home. I roughed up my hair in a spontaneous fit of anger, followed by a deep sigh of disbelief. I just turned the corner when I heard quick footsteps. They echoed louder and louder until someone grabbed my arm.

"Kale! Hold up!" I turned to see Hanna leaning against her knees struggling to breathe.

"Hi Hanna, I've been waiting for you over there. I thought you wouldn't come," I pointed.

"I know, and I am *so* sorry. Can we still go to the park?" She looked up. I saw she had red and wet eyes.

"Hanna, is everything alright?"

"Except my stamina, yeah."

"No, I'm serious."

"I just had something to deal with. Nice hair by the way." When I heard that I quickly fixed my spiky nest until it felt smooth and tidy again. I noticed she switched topics, so I went along with it without putting my nose in any personal business.

"You hungry Hanna?" I said.

"Yes, very much. There is a burger stand next to –"

" – the park." I laughed. "I planned to go there as well." After she caught her breath, we started walking. I thanked the universe that it somehow worked out in the end.

"So, I want to ask: Can you dance?" I started.

"No, not really. I hope that is okay with you."

I gave out a loud sigh, "That's great, my plan of pretending to know it all can finally burn, along with all those notes I stuck on my fridge."

"Two dance partners who cannot dance – sounds like a comedy," she said.

"A comedy I would most definitely watch!"

The conversation side tracked a million times, with multiple sidenotes, twists, and turns. The burgers and the park were the reasons we came, but the conversation was the reason we stayed. After having eaten and walked around the park, we sat down on a bench under a cherry tree, talking well through the afternoon. Its late pink blossom stood out among the oak trees nearby, fitting well with Hanna's dark dress she wore. Come to think of it, I forgot to complement her on her looks – what a complete klutz I was.

"About that dancing. Do you want to practice perhaps? During the ball I don't mind embarrassing myself in front of strangers, but they know you," she said.

I stood up, brushed off my imaginary dust off my shoulders and bowed, stretching my arm gently. "Madam, care for a dance?"

After a quick giggle, she sat up straight and accepted my offer, "Indeed I do. Would be a waste not to with such grand music."

Literally on the first step we took together, she stepped on my right foot, losing her balance off to the side. I countered it and grabbed her by her waist so she could stand. It took me a second to realise what I just did and when I did, I let go.

"Sorry," I said, keeping my hands to myself.

"I should be the one apologising." She smiled. "And the one thanking you."

Something in her smile enchanted me. I didn't know what it was, but it felt like a blanket during rainy days. Like a ringing phone after lonely weeks.

"Ok, let's try this again." She shook her head to focus. "How should I stand?"

"Not sure, but I think your left hand should be on my shoulder, and the right should rest on my palm," I answered.

I did some previous research because I never danced with a partner before - a *serious* dance, with locking hands, stiff necks and all sorts of wide steps.

At first Hanna hovered her hand over my shoulder, barely touching it, so I pressed it down.

"Don't worry," I said. "It's fine. Do the same with your other hand – yes, just like that."

"You too!" She laughed out loud.

I put my right arm on her shoulder blade.

This time she took my hand and placed it firmly on her waist. My eyes popped open in surprise, trying to stay as calm as possible. We were in position, readjusting our joints in search of comfort.

"Now what?" She asked.

"Well, now comes the dancing part. I haven't looked at any specific routines, but we could just try to move left and right first."

She counted down and we both attempted to walk to one side, holding our position as consistent as possible. Granted, I stepped on her feet twice.

"Let's go back now," she lead, slightly pulling me. That time everything went smoothly, I just kept my feet under me, not letting them wonder off too far into her direction.

I let her go, and we both broke character.

"Well, that will be fun to practice," I said sarcastically.

Hanna looked around and walked right passed me.

"Excuse me!" She said to an elderly couple sitting on another bench. "Do you know how to dance?"

The lady looked at Hanna in disbelief. "Of course, we do sweetheart. We danced together since our prom. Isn't that right William?"

The gentleman next to her nodded and stood up. He took off his blazer and folded it neatly on the hand rest of the bench. The lady took his hand.

"We will show you a couple tricks that we have learned." William said. "First of all, will you have suspenders or a belt?"

I struggled to keep up, as I was perplexed by how fast and confident Hanna asked for help.

"Belt," I said.

"Alright. In any case you *do* have suspenders, make sure their tight enough, otherwise they could slide around –"

"It happened before, and it was too funny," the lady interrupted.

"Yes Mary, very funny." He smiled at her. "Now, we had a glance at your stance, and it seems solid enough, so we won't correct you too much there. Make sure you stand comfortably, and don't strain your partner. Holding your hands too high or too far from the body are the easiest mistakes," they showed us.

They were in position so seamlessly. I couldn't see any shifting for correction, not even the fingers.

"Now, what I would recommend, and I think you do too Mary, is a free dance without too much structure," William said, taking the first steps. "The leader shows the partner what is intended. You can use the pressure on your palms to guide in order to be on the same page. Now you just go in circles, spinning around once every now and again. The rhythm depends on the music of course, but it's easy to catch. Just like so."

William began humming a song. They flowed across the dirt with grace. They ended their short performance by a goofy jump done by William.

"Forgive him, he always does that," Mary chuckled. "Now you, let's see what we have to work with."

Hanna and I took our positions.

William adjusted my arm slightly and tapped my foot so I'd spread my stance by a smidge.

"That's it. Now, who is the leader?" Mary said.

We both looked at each other without knowing the answer to that question.

"From what I saw, it should be you, young lady," William said. "Usually it's the man leading, but it's because of our ego and self-centredness."

"You're damn right," Mary sparked a little laughter.

"What you have to do is to tell your partner where you want to go. Not by saying, but by feeling," William said.

"I want to move to my right," Hanna said.

"Alright, then push, or stretch your right arm slightly, so he knows too - Yes, exactly right!" William said.

Me and Hanna slowly but surely moved along, practicing to turn and move in various directions without saying a word. At one point, I thought I felt she wanted me to go forwards, towards her, making her take a step backwards, but I got it wrong. I stepped on her foot with confidence and vigour.

"Oh, I'm so sorry," I blurted out, embracing her quickly.

"It didn't hurt too much," Hanna patted my back.

William and Mary, now leaning against the bench watching us, pitched in with a little story.

"This happened to us so often through the times. Of course, the more you do it, the less it happens," William said.

"But the best thing of all, is that from all our perfect dances, great performances, or bored evenings, we remember those moments most of all. I still remember it like it was yesterday, when William graduated from his army training, dressed up all nice and clean shaven. I could see myself in his polished shoes, but I quickly faded in them with the amount of times I stepped on his feet during our dance." Mary said.

"I still have the shoes, I never polished them again. I wore my second pair until they broke," William acknowledged.

"Aw, that is so cute." Hanna looked at them. "I hope I will turn out like you two. You're such an inspiration."

They blushed, and shrugged off the compliment.

"We once were just like you, but you are better dancers from the get go," Mary said.

William put on his blazer and they excused themselves.

"Good luck," they both said smiling, and holding each other arm in arm.

"What a blessed experience this was. Did you see how happy they were?" Hanna said to me.

I could just nod, thinking of everything they said and helped us with.

We spent some time trying to see what felt right – whether we wanted to dance stiffer or more relaxed. We didn't care about other onlookers that seemed entertained.

We danced until it got dark. The shifting of movements and balance for so long tired me out tremendously, so was the case for her.

Chapter Seven

A frantic wake a few days later, thinking it was a work or school day. It was one of those where from a good deep sleep, I burst open my eyes with a million thoughts going through my head, anxious that I was late for something. I rarely slept in, maybe it was that.

With that morning rush, even though I could have gone back to sleep, my body didn't let me. I hurled myself up, finding my trusty sliders and shuffling to the bathroom to get ready for the plans of the day – absolutely nothing. I sat on my couch in my jeans and wrinkly T-shirt, looking around my flat, seeing all the chores were done, except for the vacuuming and the ironing. But it wasn't necessary yet.

My calendar showed me that I had a few work days spread out between free days, so I couldn't get a routine in. Even worse, with the last lecture already behind me, I was running out of things to do.

In the fear of boring myself to death, and not wanting to go visit family who lived a city away, I pondered what to fill it up with.

"I could find a hobby," I said to myself out loud. "Maybe I could start painting, like Ryan does, or learn a music instrument like Ellie. Sports? No, I really don't want to do that."

There was nothing I wanted to do. Nothing waiting for me out there that screamed my name. Heck, I couldn't even trace a whisper.

Looking at my calendar again I spotted the upcoming date of the ball. After having eaten some buttered toast, I opened my closet and took out everything that was worthy to be worn for the ball; Shirts, ties, trousers, fancy shoes, belts, jewellery. With the music blaring from my phone, I tried all the articles on. I discovered that I didn't like any shirts I owned, with some being too baggy, and some just plain ugly.

"Have I lost weight?" I asked myself, pinching the roll of fat under my belly button. "I just might have," I said looking in the mirror.

I found a pair of trousers that were fine, but I decided to buy some new ones for the occasion. I had some money saved up from the job, and thinking I would be working more anyway, I didn't feel bad of spending a little.

I needed a shirt, trousers, a shoe polisher and maybe a blazer. After all this preparation for the dancing, I couldn't show up not looking the best I could.

It was drizzling outside, so I took an umbrella my friend left behind before he left to his hometown for the summer. I was checking my phone for directions to a relatively cheap tailor. I found one that was conveniently in the shopping mall, so I didn't have to worry about the rain for long.

The squeaky-clean white tiles, together with the white walls and ceiling made it look 'too clean'. The only thing that stood out were the people, the branding, and the items in them. Even the benches and seats were white.

"Hello," I said to the tailor who was sitting behind his desk all by himself.

"Good day to you." He stood up. "What do you need? Formal, or casual? Cheap or pricy? And most importantly, dress to impress, or to blend in?"

"Ehm – Formal and cheap. Not sure what the last one means, but I don't want to be too flamboyant."

"I hear you." He circled around his desk.

"I would be looking for a full suit with a shirt that fits well but isn't too tight."

"Of course, right here I can see some that you can try on. You are rather tall, so I have to see that the shirt isn't too short, or too wide."

He looked through hangers with shirts. To me they all looked the same, so I wasn't sure what he was looking for. The sizes seemed very similar as well.

He plucked one out and handed it to me.

"Now let's go here and pick out your colour of the suit. These are the cheapest in the store, with those ones over there being a bit pricier, but still good value. I would go for black, the classic."

I nodded.

He did the same thing again, looked for a good size and plucked one out. I was surprised he didn't ask me for my size at all, but he seemed to know what he was doing, and with him being so confident, I didn't want to interfere with his process. He did the same with the trousers.

"I know you didn't say you wanted shoes, but I will give you a pair just so you can see how the suit looks with a pair of shoes on. You have black shoes, right?" He said, showing me the way to the fitting rooms.

I nodded again. "I want to have them polished. Thinking of it, I also need shoe polish."

"I will write it up for you, no problem. One last thing, I can see you have black socks, make sure you wear black socks during the event. No branding - smooth socks that will always cover your ankles, so they have to be long enough. Also, they must – and that is my pet peeve – they must not roll down."

It was all so much information that he bombarded me with, but he seemed to be a decent guy, genuinely trying to help me out.

I started changing, and while I was putting my trousers on, he slid a pair of sparkly shoes under the curtain. When I got ready, I presented myself.

"Alright! That's a good start, but I can see a couple faults instantly." He looked at me with one of his hands caressing his beard, and the other resting on his hip.

It didn't seem to me that there was something wrong at all, I was quite pleased in fact.

"The collar is a tad too tight, the trousers a smidgen too long – but we can fix that. But you know what disturbs me the most?"

I looked at him confused.

"Your face!" He said disappointingly. "You are not happy, and I cannot allow that. Wearing a suit is all about presentation. You can have the most expensive, rarest suit in the world, but without a smile to capture all of that, it all goes to waste. Now go back and get undressed. I'll hand you the corrections now."

He rushed off, getting swallowed whole by the tons of hanging clothes. We tried again and during the second presentation I could feel the difference.

"Better, right?" He asked.

"Yes! Much better, thank you!" I looked down at my ankles without the collar choking me. Coming to think of it, maybe I never had a well fitted suit before. Maybe all of them were a bit too tight, too loose, or just worn down by my dad.

"We are not done yet, not by a long shot," the tailor said. "Come with me."

He showed me a large shelf overlain with glass so I could see all the jewellery, ties, and all sorts of things.

"Now, what sparks your interest in this area?"

I pointed towards a pair of silver *things* in a shape of anchors. "They seem cool."

"These are cufflinks, to fasten your shirt around your wrist. See those holes?"

I began to feel stupid.

"Now here, what tie is either interesting to you, or closest to what you have already, so we can see what it would look like. I recommend any of these shades, they work well with what you have on already."

"Ok, this one looks eerily similar to one I have, and this one is the prettiest in my opinion."

"I hear you," he takes those out.

"Can I have the honour of picking out the pocket square? It goes to your pocket *here*", he patted me on the chest lightly.

"Eh, sure why not."

"Oh, thank you so much!"

I also picked out a belt which went well with my jewellery. I also had my watch on. He helped me equip all those things, readjusting the position of the pocket square multiple times, until he uttered the word 'perfect'.

"I don't want to be rude young sir," he then said, scanning me up and down.

"No, please, it's fine. What is it?"

"Your watch. It doesn't fit with the colour scheme. It's a bit - how should I say it - *off-putting*."

I turned to see myself in the mirror and indeed it was a bit glaring. But I liked it, it was different and attracted the eye.

"I think I like it. A bit of crazy in a classy suit," I said.

"Of course, you are the master of your appearance. When it comes to me you are finished. The hair will be stylised more accurately I'm sure, so other than that you look fabulous!"

He wasn't wrong. I felt like I could star in a restaurant series, full of celebrities and dishes that cost more than my rent.

"And do you see it?" he asked.

"See what?"

"Something that I am looking for in everyone who steps through the door. The smile."

I looked up to see my teeth exposed and eyes full of pride.

"Do you want to take it?" He asked.

Of course. I bought all the things I needed, and the tailor even gave me a discount. What a nice man.

"Enjoy your occasion sir," he handed me the bag.

"Thank you so much."

I spent a long time at home looking at the things I bought and hanging them with care.

"I hope Hanna will like it" I said to myself.

The time for the ball finally arrived. The days leading up to this were filled with anxiety, even though it shouldn't have been such a big deal. But when I woke up on the day, this anxiety transformed into a mixture of things; excitement, nervousness, ecstasy, and probably terror. I wasn't sure at the time, but my unsteady hands should have given me enough insight into how I felt.

Having taken a long shower, washing my hair thoroughly and styling it just right, I took out my freshly prepared suit and put all its individual bits and bobs on my bed. I tried the newly bought things on. It took me a fairly long time, but I finally managed.

The closer it got to my "get out the house" alarm, the more I rushed. By the end, I left without having eaten anything, but looking on point. I made my way to Hanna's place finally, tiptoeing on streets not to ruin my polished shoes, swerving around obstacles not to damage the flower bouquet in my hands that I bought earlier the same day.

The closer I got to her place the more my stomach protested. I slowly felt nauseous, which was the biggest worry to be entirely honest.

"Come on man, you can do this. She likes you already, what are you worried about?" I said to myself. "I can do this. I can do this. I can do this..." I repeated.

Her door suddenly appeared in front of me. When I realised it, I took a deep breath and just went for it, throwing myself into deep waters and nerves going haywire. I rang the bell and just stood there with the bouquet right in front of me.

The door opened, revealing a girl in a hoodie and jeans.

"*You Kale?*" She said, obviously judging me, looking up and down.

When I nodded, she just walked away from the door.

"Hanna, Kale is here!" She shouted up the stairs. Then she just walked in a room and shut the door behind her, which radiated loud rock music.

I just stood by the entrance door not knowing what I should be doing. "Come on man, calm down," I whispered to myself.

The hallway was all white, with all sorts of decorations. You could immediately tell that the people that did it had an idea of what they were doing. A chain of framed photographs of many different people hung on the wall. I looked at them, slowly, one-by-one, until I reached the end of the hallway.

"What you looking at?" Hanna startled me. For a split second I didn't recognise her. She wore a red flannel dress that fit her wonderfully. I learned that it was smooth to the touch and well made. Her hair was cut to shoulder length, which framed her fantastic smile perfectly.

"You look beautiful," I didn't dare to look her in the eyes.

To my surprise she caught me in a tight hug. "Thank you so much, Kale." I let the flowers drop to the floor and embraced her too.

I wished it would last just a little bit longer. A warmth came over me, as her breath imitated mine. It just felt as if our hearts were beating in sync, becoming one.

"I brought you flowers," I said in the state of bliss contentedness.

"I saw," she whispered in my ear.

I picked them up from the floor and gave them to her. She took them and quickly left to the kitchen.

"We do have time, don't we?" Her voice bounced around to the hallway.

"Yes, don't worry. By the way, we will be walking there, is that okay?"

Upon hearing that, she flew back into the hallway with the same energy as in the café.

"Thank you," she said.

"Than- Thank me for what?"

"For deciding which shoes to take." She giggled while putting on a pair of sneakers that fit the colour scheme of her dress.

We went out and turned left as soon as we passed her gate. The perfume that I decided to wear fused with hers, as we walked side by side on a worn pavement of a busy street.

"I am quite nervous," she turned to me, bumping our shoulders. "I don't know what to expect."

"It's a ball. I think we are not the only ones that are nervous."

"You might be right, anyway, how many of them would have spent their time practicing dance moves?" She giggled again.

"That is true. I will probably forget some bits, so I will seem like the odd one of us two," I said.

"Nonsense! I will be the first one to make a mistake."

I stopped in my tracks and reached out my arm. She looked at me inquisitively, "You *wanna* bet?"

She grasped my palm firmly and shook it. "So be it." Her eyebrows shifted from round and cute, to being sharp and full of vigour. I guess we had a challenge of some sort which would doom us to fail.

"At least when we do embarrass ourselves, we can still win something," we continued the walk.

When we reached a large crossroad, we found a few more people dressed elegantly waiting to cross. There was one guy who had too short trousers. When standing, we could see his socks rather well. They popped out enthusiastically, as one was bright red, and the other was turquoise. Very strange, but oddly fun.

I knew Hanna spotted them too when she turned away to keep her laugh in check.

When the loud beeping noise of the green light revealed itself, we crossed in a small group, all heading towards a large grey building. It had white windows that were tall and had square panes. One of the double doors was already open, with a sign in front of it saying:

Welcome to the Summer Ball!
Student IDs required.

Cloakroom to the right.

When we entered the reception area, I could smell the food being prepared. I felt my stomach rage for it, but unfortunately it needed to wait. After a considerable queuing wait, we finally gave our things to the cloakroom staff. We got a flimsy little piece of paper that would usually get buried into my back pocket. It was those things that disintegrated in my washing machine after having forgotten them. Tiny bits of paper flaking all the clothes.

"I will take those." She grabbed my paper out of my hand and put it into her purse.

"Kale!" someone shouted from the back of the queue somewhere. "Kale!" I heard once more, but this time I saw a couple squeeze past.

"Roland! Trina! How amazing you both look," I suddenly felt elated.

"So do both of you." Trina went to hug me and then Hanna.

"Well, someone is excited. Like a puppy when you come back home after a long day." Roland smiled mischievously, knowing that Trina would wind up a big punch on the shoulder. Indeed, it was a hard hit.

"We weren't sure where to sit, but now that you're here, we will wait for you to leave your jackets," Hanna suggested.

"Let's jump right back in then," Roland joined the queue once more.

While we waited, we looked around the place. The building was not connected to the university in any way. It was a corporate building. Through the bustle of people walking around, I caught a glimpse of the hall. It was massive! I even saw a chandelier, as well as a side balcony where one could look over the entire hall.

"It is massive," I blurted out in awe.

"Yeah… it's quite unnerving," Hanna tried not to look. Instead, she tried to see how Roland and Trina were moving along.

It took a while. I took a big breath when we entered through the tall walls and pillars, into the hall. The glints of the chandeliers, of which there were eight, blinded me for a moment. The walls were of creamy stone, marvellously engraved. The floor was out of white tiles, with each tile being bigger than my own body. The hall was surrounded by a balcony that had thick stone balustrade railings, which were evenly separated by a post in form of horses. There were round tables placed all over, with eight seats on each table. They were covered in a white tablecloth, on which were sets of plates, cutlery, glasses and flowers in the centre.

"Where should we go?" Trina said worryingly.

"No tables are completely empty, so we need to ask if we can join any of them," I pointed out.

After shuffling along, we had found a table with enough space left for all four of us. The four others were dressed very traditionally. The boys were sitting uptight seemingly for the whole evening. Their hair was pulled back so hard, it must have been uncomfortable for them. The girls wore similar dresses and talked with each other the whole evening, rarely acknowledging our presence. Throughout the ball, they did not go dance a single time.

It took forever for the food to arrive. Luckily, I was the first one to be served of all of us at the table. The waiter hardly put the plate down, and I already attacked the fish with my fork and knife.

"*Hoo* buddy, you won't wait for us?" Hanna asked.

I couldn't answer, as half of my dish was already in my mouth.

"He likes to eat." Roland took the words out of my mouth, or rather the fish in this instance.

The waiter came back for the rest of us, but by that point I was chewing on the last bits of my dish. The waiter's face...

the disgust and judgement towards me was uncanny. I extinguished my hunger a bit, and the fish was astonishing.

"Well, I like to drink," Hanna laughed, opening a beer bottle that she sneakily took from the self-service with a bottle opener from a well-used keychain.

"Handy!" Trina said, springing up and quickly making her way to the table full of liquor.

So, there it was, the long-awaited ball of the year, with me, Hanna, Roland, and Trina sitting on a round table savouring the all-you-can-eat buffet and the endless supply of various alcohol. We did use that privilege rather well before the headmaster's speech on the stage far away in the front of the hall.

"Good evening, everyone!" He said. "I hope I can take a moment of your precious evening to say a few words."

With the hall being so big, I could hear a lot of murmurs around. Having so many people in one place, it would be impossible for a quiet environment. It was bugging me somewhat.

With heavy breaths and crackling noises of the paper he was holding, presumably very tightly, he continued, "Given that everyone here has finished their exams, I want to congratulate you for attending and trying your best this year. I hope you can find some rest during your vacation. I cannot say the same for the wonderful staff, that have a mammoth job on their hands grading all the papers. Good luck to you." Laughing and chuckling echoed within the walls. "On a more organisational note, we will have an official three course meal, that all of you have already started eating. After which, there will be a self-service buffet on the right side throughout the rest of the evening for those who feel more peckish. We also have liquor available, but please try to drink responsibly. Thank you to all the waiters and waitresses, chefs, and staff for making all of this possible, and again, applause to everyone who made it here. Have a great night!"

The large applause was a sign for the DJ to begin his set that would last well into the next day. Everything erupted. People stood up, walking around. The chatter and laughter began its cycle - the music deafening any silence in between.

We also contributed to the chatter and soon enough we loosened up.

"Kale! What about a shot of this?" Roland handed me a small glass of transparent liquid.

"What is this?" I asked, not entirely sure.

"Alcohol."

"No way, I would have never thought." I looked at him with fake surprise and sarcasm. "I mean what kind? I want to know what I will be trying."

Even though all of them seemed sceptical, their intrigued postures felt supportive, especially Hanna and her gentle stare.

"It's vodka." Trina lifted an identical glass, as well did the other two. "Cheers!"

I wasn't sure if I would be doing it, to be entirely honest. However, everyone was going for it with the expectation that I would be joining them, so by peer pressure I presume, I downed it.

"Hey!" Roland shouted out. "I don't know you like *this* at all! Congrats to you!"

Through squinted eyes and the exact same horrific taste as I remembered, I heard all three having a small cheer for me. It must've looked so sad from the outside, but I enjoyed it.

"It's horrendous, but don't be expecting for me to go further tonight," I said.

"Don't worry, we won't be pressuring you for another just yet," Roland winked at me.

"Don't drink if you don't want to," Hanna countered Roland. "But is it alright with you if I drink somewhat more?"

I never had a problem with people drinking in front of me, so naturally I went along with it. She was already in her third round by this time, so it wouldn't have made any difference. But it was nice of her to ask anyway.

Their drinking continued, and I drank too, giving in to the occasion. Roland's storytelling amused us as well as all Trina's corrections. I always admired her knack of remembering details. Stories of his expense, and sometimes mine too. Hanna listened intently and asked questions from time to time. Having eaten the last meal of the course, Trina's fork screeched on her plate.

"I am full," she said.

"Wow, that is a rare occurrence." Roland received a laser look from her.

"Anyway, Hanna, can you tell something about yourself? You had to listen to all this, but I still know you as the waitress of that café," Trina continued.

I laughed, but I was curious too. Maybe Trina waited for me to ask but grew impatient. I would have never dared, so good that she did.

"What do you want to know?" Hanna said between a spoonful of soup that she got herself from the self-serving buffet.

Trina gave me a daring look.

"Actually – I would be curious if you have any pets," I jumped in. Roland hid his facepalm extremely well from Hanna. Trina scoffed.

"Well, that's a question I didn't expect. But yes, I have a fish."

"Oh wow, what kind?" Roland jumped excitedly.

"A Siamese fighting fish. She is quite timid, but I love her. She is two and a half years old, so she is beginning to be an old lady."

"Oh man… I wish we could have pets…" Roland looked at Trina.

"Oh yes, so they can die as soon as you get them. You will forget to feed them all the time! I will be the one who will have to check up on them, which I quite frankly don't want to do." Trina blurted out, as if she was waiting for her cue. "I love them, don't get me wrong, but right now would be horrible timing, and inconvenient."

I slurped my glass of water and looked awkwardly away.

"Thanks, Trina, for exposing me like that." Roland shrugged in embarrassment. "Do you have any pictures of him? I don't know what that Simis fish is."

Hanna put her glass down and took out her phone from her purse. "It's S-i-a-m-e-s-e. They differ in colour, mine is white."

Hanna turned the screen towards him, showing him a picture.

"Woah, Trina look! It's so beautiful," Roland's chin dropped.

"She is called Luna."

When Hanna showed me as well, I was struck by the beauty of Luna. It was so majestic and flawless. It reminded me of the feeling I got when I saw some of my butterflies. It was weird. I used to get such a deep appreciation that I was allowed to witness such grace and vulnerability. It was… "truly amazing."

"Yes, she is," Trina responded.

"Other than that, I had a dog as a child, but it is now with my brother." Hanna put her phone back into her purse.

"Oh, I have two sisters! I would love to have a brother." I started tapping my foot in excitement.

"No, you wouldn't…" Hanna finished off her beer and stood up. "I'm going to get another beer, anyone want anything?"

They both declined, and everyone looked at me. Roland stared at me and pointed at Hanna with his eyes, very strikingly.

"I-I will join you," I followed Roland's orders.

"Great!" she took my arm so that I wouldn't lose her amidst all the dancers and roamers. We zigzagged through them. As I looked at her, my knees felt a bit weak, and my mind was fuzzy. It was a long time since I was last drunk. Her black hair was held up by the same pin she used during work. The quick movements became a blur, and suddenly all the people we weaved through transformed into chairs and tables. The chandelier above fused its shiny bits into one striking warmth of the sun. Everything changed, except for her red flannel dress that flailed in motion. I could nearly smell the coffee and taste the brownie, so tender it melted in the mouth.

"- as well?" Hanna disrupted my trail of thought.

"Sorry?"

"Do you want a beer as well?" She held two bottles.

"Actually, I might go for one. But I will drink it slowly."

"We haven't danced yet. All the practice would have been for nothing. If you'd be up for it, we could go soon – maybe with another song," she said.

That was a surprise, but I wasn't really against it. So, I agreed. We turned to the dancefloor and looked at how everybody was doing. There were a couple of good dancers out there, and the flamboyant, and those that only had one dance move in their repertoire. The song genre varied, but mostly consisted of pop or mild rock. The modern as well as the classics. Every now and then the DJ put some romantic songs too, where only those in pairs kept on dancing.

"Looks like fun," I lied.

"Yeah, we will join them in the next song," she took more and more sips.

I just hoped that I could summon my inner disco soul that Trina unlocked back at Roland's party. I tried to remember what she had told me.

We waited until the song ended. We took the alcohol to our table. I saw three girls finely dressed with long wavy hair that must have been meticulously styled.

"Hello! How wonderful you all look!" I said.

They turned around and Ellie came in for a hug.

"Hi Kale! Nice to see you again!"

I wasn't sure why but I did not embrace her. I just let my hands hover over her with a bottle in each hand. I cringed as Hanna just went passed us directly to the table.

"Is that your date?" Ellie said out loud so everyone could hear.

I could feel my face turn red and I wasn't sure what to say.

"Ehm. She is not really –"

"Yes, that's me! I'm Hanna, nice to meet you." Hanna responded with cold blood. They shook hands and started to talk, Ellie enthusiastically, but Hanna remained calm.

"That was a win right there, *man*." Roland appeared beside me and took one of the bottles out of my hand. "But try to loosen up. I don't know how you do it, I know you're a bit tipsy, but you're still so uptight."

"I'm not nervous," I said in a low tone.

"I didn't say you were. The bottles are not cooled or anything, but they sure are slippery," Roland hid his smile. He thought he was funny, but he knew exactly what I was going through.

"What should I do exactly?"

"Come here," he took me in closer and spoke directly into my ear.

"Spend more time alone with her. She has been doing everything, *leading* in some sense. Take some initiative and go tell her you're going to dance."

After he released me from his strong grip, I went straight to Hanna and interrupted her conversation.

"Let's go!" I jumped at her. "The songs are better now."

"Oh, someone sprung from a fiery bush!" Hanna laughed. I never heard that expression before, but it was accurate. "I'm sorry, but it seems we *must* go. But I want to come back to this conversation," she said to Ellie.

And just like that I was leading her onto the dancefloor, a place we so feared. When we got there, we found ourselves a pocket of space.

I had Trina's voice in my head and did what she told me. I closed my eyes and took in the heavy bass through the vibrating floor. I swayed a little at first, but gradually I grew more confident. I used the bright lights that penetrated my closed eyes to let myself drift away. The red spots dotted around every now and again, like sprayed droplets. The Blues were smudged all around, slithering from one place to the next. Lastly, the Greens covered the whole darkness with its faintness.

I did let myself go, maybe even too much. Our spot was big enough so that I didn't feel anyone bumping into me or strafing me during their dance moves. I was all alone in my own world. A straggler among dancers, who was present, but far away from everyone.

But when someone bumped into me from the back, I opened my eyes to see if everything was alright. I saw Hanna stare right at me. I could tell she was deep in thought. Another bump, this time a lot harder, made me step closer to her. She took me in for a hug. She didn't say anything, neither did she have to. Her hair sat on my shoulder, tickling my neck. Her cheek pressed against mine tightly, slowing down both our breaths.

I lifted my head away from hers. It was at this point I knew what I wanted to do, probably for a long time. She waited for me, but as soon as I began nearing myself to her again, the music changed to a slow rhythmic song and all the colours that enchanted me were erased. Suddenly, I was sober again, and so I just stayed planted, frozen.

"Do you want to dance?" Hanna's smile drifted away.

"Oh, of course!"

I expected her to come closer to me, so we could begin, but she expected *me* to initiate. Everyone around us either went to their tables already or were well into the dance. We just stood there motionless.

"Won't you take my hand?" Hanna frowned slightly.

To be honest, I didn't know what I was thinking. I felt so embarrassed that I wanted to leave this whole thing altogether and lay in my bed to stare at my white ceiling. And while I thought of that, Hanna lifted my hand from beside me, and forcefully made us take the first steps.

"Don't worry Kale. Look at it this way – you won the bet," she told me. "Now just relax and do what we practiced. Slowly."

I tried to focus only on her, as with every sharp turn we took, I could see from the corner of my eye that a ring of people developed, watching the few dancers. When I saw Roland's obvious tie, I glanced at him. He stood proudly, like a dad seeing his child do well in sports. Trina stood next to him, and so did the three girls with their partners.

"You're doing well," Hanna said.

"Don't know what I'm doing really, you are leading the way."

"Just do whatever you've been doing so far. It's working… I think."

When she said that, my hands loosened up, letting her palm breathe and float on top of mine. I stretched my neck upwards and took a deep breath with my chest out. All I needed to do was the presentation, the actual dancing was on Hanna. It was funny, because we were so afraid of this moment, and now we seemed to enjoy it. She didn't look at me one bit, but always slightly beside me, as if she was scanning the people around us.

"The song is ending I think," I said, as there was a noticeable drop of instruments playing, leaving the piano and violin play in a calm duet.

And as the last notes were played, we stopped. I did a goofy jump. Hanna laughed out loud, which made me giggle too. To my surprise, we were the only ones left in the ring, and an applause erupted all around.

"Like a pro!" Roland screamed out, over the noise of everyone's clapping. Then a lot of whistling ensued, and sure enough a crowd of guys, led by no other than Roland, surrounded me and chanted, alienating Hanna in the process.

"*Bro*, that was awesome."

"You got some balls."

"A bit stiff but for sure will do nicely."

And on and on came the comments, with pats on the back and more cheering. A hip-hop song erupted through the speakers and we all jumped up and down like a wave in tune of that absolute classic. Everyone else had joined in, and I got lost in the crowd once more.

A few songs went by, and I decided it was enough for me, as my collar turned to a cold, wet mess, and so did my back. I took a breather for the sake of my shirt. My gel also dripped down my forehead. In the meantime, I would get a drink as well.

"Where is Hanna?" I asked Ellie who was at our table.

"She went outside. She said she will come back soon. Incredible dance by the way! Where did you learn this? I was so jealous I couldn't dance with my partner." She leaned towards me and covered her mouth somewhat. "He is not too fun."

I laughed out loud. "It's a complicated story, but Trina taught me the basics."

I then left with a bottle of beer and some juice to look for Hanna. As I stepped out, the fresh wind welcomed me immediately, chilling every sweaty inch. But it was good to get out of the humid, sticky air for once. I saw Hanna on the other side of the street, sitting on the kerb smoking a cigarette.

"I didn't know you smoked," I handed her the beer. "Oh, I forgot to open it!" I turned back to get the bottle opener.

"It's fine! I'll handle it," she said, opening the bottle from the kerb's edge in one swing. "There you go!" She smiled.

I sat down next to her. "That was a surreal experience, don't you think? I never felt so… so…"

"In the moment," she nodded.

"Exactly! I never knew we were alone, until the very end. I'm sorry for the awkward beginning though!"

We both erupted in laughter and sipped our drinks. When our echoes died down, we could only hear the muffled music from the hall. We saw people coming and going. Some went out to go home, others just for some fresh air. Friends or family waiting in cars to pick some of them up. The moon shone through the thin clouds.

Hanna squished her cigarette butt on the kerb. "So, Kale…," she said, not drunk, but tipsy for sure. "Why did you ask me?"

"What do you mean?"

"Why did you ask *me* to go here with you? From what I saw and heard you had a lot of friends to go with."

"Does it really look like that?" I thought out loud. "I'm not really the popular one, you know."

"I don't think so. You seem to have a lot of attention."

"Maybe now, but normally the library is my best friend."

"That's not true, is it?" Hanna didn't let up. "They all love you."

I started fidgeting with my shoelaces. "I would rather pass by busy streets completely unknown."

"Why?"

"Well… You see, when I was younger, I made many promises. These promises I held very dear. They would repeat in my head from the moment I woke up to the last thought of the night. Like jars with fish inside them I would keep them alive. But, once I let other people see them, the fish would die one after the other, sometimes the jars would be smashed to pieces. Imagine you come home one day and Luna would be gone, and you know someone was behind it. You wouldn't trust anyone near your fish ever again."

I could feel Hanna leaning her head on my shoulder. I took her hand.

"Wow… I didn't expect that. I'm sorry," she said faintly.

"Nothing to be sorry about, it's just unfortunate really." After a moment of thinking I broke the silence anew. "But what makes me wonder, is not why I asked you, but why you accepted."

"That I won't tell. You can puzzle it together yourself." Her hand began shaking, and her legs weren't still either.

"Are you cold?" I made her sit up.

"No, but I will be right back."

She stood up, brushed the red flannel dress off and began walking. In the middle of the street, she turned back and grabbed her purse that she forgot next to me.

I plucked out some weeds that grew in the cracks of the pavement. I twisted them, peeled and broke them into smaller pieces, until my palm was filled with a mix of dirt and shredded greenery. I was daydreaming.

"-ey!" Hanna clapped her hands right in front of me. "That was a deep thought. *What you thinking?*"

She seemed much more drunk, maybe too much at that point.

"Oh, nothing." I threw away whatever was in my hands and stood up. "Are you alright?"

"Yeah, I think. Roland asked about you, I think we should go back."

We did. I sobered up a little and saw the hall for what it was. Everyone was much more relaxed. There were a handful of professors left, but they were ready to leave. The dancefloor was emptier than at any point of the night. The music that blared were unedited pop songs, because the DJ was at his table taking a well-deserved break, or maybe even thinking of leaving himself.

When I scanned the place, Roland popped out and walked straight towards me.

"Kale! I was worried you dipped already." He came for a hug, stumbling and reeking of booze.

Trina, trying to help him keep his balance, said, "We are leaving. It was a lovely night, but the party is dying down really quickly."

"Oh," I said, "I wish you a good night's sleep then." I laughed, but I was quite disappointed. It was good for him in hindsight, he was really struggling.

As they left, Hanna and I went to our table to find it empty, but filled with partly eaten snacks on plates, glasses of alcohol, and for some reason, the decorative flower out of its vase.

"Ahh, no wonder they left." Hanna inspected the table too.

I thought about it and concluded that the time for us was over too. Hanna agreed, and so we were walking back with our jackets. At the crossroads, Hanna opened up her jacket partly and took out two bottles of beer out of the inner pockets.

"Ta da!" she laughed.

"I think I had enough today," I said.

"All this to surprise you, and you decline? That's mean." She went right instead of straight, sitting down on a bench. "Come sit!" Her voice echoed in the empty streets.

I didn't want to, but just so she could tone down her voice, I did as she said. I didn't want to be one of the annoying drunks that woke people up.

"Alright, I'm here. What now?"

"Tell me." She already opened her bottle and started sipping. "Why are you so afraid?"

"What do you mean?"

"To tell me that you like me." She put the bottle down.

I didn't know what to say. I could feel my face turn red again. I froze. "Ehm… I –"

"Or maybe that you *really* like me." She shuffled closer to me and kissed me on the cheek.

I felt the same as during the dance. It was incredible.

She looked deep into my eyes. "You're different. I knew from the first time I saw you in the café."

I wanted to kiss her back, but didn't know how to do it, so I launched for a tight hug.

"I will take it as a yes," she said.

I could feel her heart was beating fast, and her breath was very irregular. I looked at her again and decided I had to get her home. So, I helped her up and we stumbled our way to her home. Every now and then we had to stop for a break. Whenever a car passed by, they slowed down to look at us, but we were fine.

She leaned on her mailbox when I struggled to get her door open with the keys she gave me. But once I have finally done it, I helped her to her room. She faceplanted onto her bed, giggling into the pillow. I closed the door to not wake up her flatmates and turned the light on.

Her room was creative. In one corner there were origami shapes hanging from the ceiling on strings. A bulletin board with loads of pictures and drawings. Quite cozy, much better than my whole flat. Her bed had too many pillows though, they would only annoy me.

I put on her light on the nightstand and tucked her in. I leaned over and told her that I would be leaving.

"No," Hanna was breathing heavily. "Please stay with me, you lovely boy."

"I will leave you alone. We can meet up tomorrow if you want."

"No…" she looked at me smiling drunkenly. "Alright… if you need to go, then go. But give me a kiss."

I did, and my heart filled up immediately when our lips touched.

"Goodnight," I said.

She frowned but closed her eyes. On my way to her door, I saw a big fish tank with Luna swimming around. It looked right at me. I turned the main light off and struggled home. Halfway to my house I saw on my phone that Hanna sent me a voice message, but I told myself I would listen to it at home.

In my filthy suit, covered in sweat, I stumbled into my apartment, slamming the door behind me in search for rest. When I finally hit the sheets, the duvet, the pillows, I felt like on a boat, rocking on gentle waves in the burning sunshine. I had no energy to close the blinds, nor to curse at the robins who have long started their concert. In the slow drift into my dreams, I realised that all this time I was lonely, because that day I finally felt that I had a purpose. In my drunken haze I dreamt vividly:

I woke to see myself laying against cold rocks in a cave. My hair felt damp, and my skin smooth. The walls buzzed in a high pitch, illuminating a purplish light, just about strong enough for me to see my surroundings. I stood up awkwardly and felt a tear rise up my cheek back into my eye. Out of my right pocket I took out a big white feather, and as soon as I did, I began walking backwards slowly. I stared at the feather; it was trance-like. The further I walked backwards, the colder it got. Little water droplets started to rise from the ground and my hands. The further I retreated, the more droplets appeared, until I turned around. In front of me, a massive waterfall claimed its presence. Its water that flew upwards from a pit right in front of me echoed a deep and everlasting note. The feather began to levitate off my hand rising in a rocking motion, until it reached the high ceiling, not out of rock, but what seemed to be thick roots. There the feather got stuck, among others that hung upside down.

The water kept rising and I just stood there. A stroke of my head proved my hair to be much drier. From under me something grew out of the rock that turned out to be a bench, on which I sat on swiftly. It was made of dark wood displaying an engraved pattern that seemed too complex to figure out. When I looked up towards the rising wall of the waterfall, behind it stood a dark figure.

Chapter Eight

My sticky eyes opened when a family passed by, hearing their conversation. I slept into the afternoon. I had to smash my eyes open to see through the blurry grogginess. Hanna returned to my thoughts. It was a feeling of total bliss. I stretched out all my limbs and turned to the other side, but when I did, I saw my phone light up.

I had many notifications, which I expected. I read them, barely holding on to the phone, and once I actually understood what I read, the phone dropped onto the hardwood floor, cracking its screen entirely. I retrieved it into my pocket and ran into the living room, grabbing my wallet and keys. I ran out still in my suit and dress shoes towards the city centre. On the way there I ran through all red lights, nearly getting hit by a semi-truck. I splashed through puddles, jumped kerbs, and took every shortcut necessary. When I went through the sliding doors, I knew I arrived at my destination. The bright lights and white walls blinded me and worsened my pulsing headache. I was panting hard, my veins on my arms popped and sweat started to mix with the gel and trundle down my face again.

"Where is room 77?" I shouted out at the secretary office, ignoring the long line before it.

A woman in scrubs came to me in a rush and attempted to calm me down. "Sir, are you Kale?" She showed me Hanna's phone.

"Yes! Now where is she?" I demanded to know, looking around for the room numbers. Two security guards came over to inspect what was going on, but the nurse reassured them that everything was fine.

She pointed at a corridor, "it's that way."

I ran towards it, nearly slipping on the clean floor tiles. The stairs were quickly dealt with, including the sharp corners in the hallway. When I found the number on a door matching 77, I opened the door. Still panting, I saw an empty room, except for one bed. When the doors closed behind me, there was absolute silence - I could hear my own heartbeat.

Hanna was laying there motionless. The machines on the side were off, but the tubes were still there. The room was spinning, and I lost balance, so I leaned heavily onto the windowsill.

The nurse stood by me, standing in my mist of alcohol-stricken cloud. "I'm sorry Kale, we did everything we could. You were the last contact on her phone, so we let you know."

So many questions tortured me, holding me in chains. "How long has she been gone?"

"Approximately an hour".

I thought I had control, but my mouth twitched open involuntarily. The nurse hugged me tightly, and when she did, the first tears of many started to fall.

"How could this happen? Everything was great yesterday." I cried out. The nurse didn't say anything, but I could hear her running nose.

"Tell me please, why did she…?" I insisted.

"Do you want to know now?" She broke the hug.

"Yes, please." I wiped my face.

"I don't know if you know, but she was on drugs."

"No, I didn't. What does it have to do with anything?"

"Combined with the alcohol it resulted in a stroke. She overdosed. When she was admitted to hospital, it was too late."

"This is bullshit. Bullshit!" I punched the windowsill repeatedly. "I drank with her, and everything was alright! When we left the party, she was okay! How do you know she was on drugs?"

"We tested. Plus, we found a used bottle of pills in her purse." Her pager went off. "I'll leave you alone with her, is that alright Kale?" She held on to my shoulder. After I answered her question with silence, she rushed out of the room, and it was quiet again.

I couldn't look at Hanna – not like this. There was nothing else to catch my attention besides her. I was looking for anything, just anything – flickering of the lights, the buzz of working lightbulbs, the loud flush from the toilets nearby. But nothing…

"Come on *man*, now is not the time." I started to talk to myself. "Just look at her damnit!"

My vision was all blurry, so I had to constantly wipe my eyes. I took a deep breath and looked at her.

She looked peaceful. Her neutral face smiled slightly, which I just noticed then. Her hand, that I picked up, was still warm and soft. But it wasn't the same. It felt empty.

I didn't have to say anything, and even if I wanted to, I wouldn't have the means. Looking at her, I couldn't give out a single peep.

The door opened.

"Who are you? Get away!" A man shouted at me, grabbing my collars and hurtling me across the room. I smashed against a shelf. His face radiated hatred and anger, which I understood because I felt the same. He stood over me, delivering one solid punch across my face.

I heard many distorted voices, some high pitched, some low. One of them was from the nurse earlier. "-ight?"

I inhaled through gritted teeth.

"Are you alright?" I heard her say, inspecting my face.

Behind her I saw security pull the man out the room. "What is that stranger doing next to my daughter! Can't you see, he is drunk out his mind! Let me go!"

I sat up. At this point the room was spinning again. I turned away from the nurse and puked on the floor, then everything went dark.

I woke up with beeping sounds all around, laying in a hospital bed. I couldn't lift a finger, but my mind was sharper than it was before. My clothes were gone and all I had was a hospital gown.

"Don't worry, all this was just precautionary. You blacked out with a mild concussion." I jumped in shock. Another nurse stood by my side, that I somehow didn't see. "You'll be out in a few hours, just rest for a while."

I didn't say anything.

"As soon as something is wrong: you feel pain, you feel sick, whatever, press this button. I will come to help you out," she showed me.

She walked out my prison cell. My mind was blank, but everything came back to me swiftly – the ball, the drinking, the punch, Hanna. The ceiling was my only friend.

'What the hell is happening?' I asked it in my mind. It didn't respond and left my thoughts drift through the nothingness. I counted the imperfections on the ceiling. Wave-like little bumps.

One thing after another began to piss me off. The folds of the sheets dug into my hips, the hard pillow made my neck sore, and worst of all, the duvet was tucked in so tightly, I couldn't get set my feet free. All I could think was what could be worse, and nothing came to mind, which made my hands tremble, and the darkness of my closed eyes seemed as if I was floating in a void of incomparable misery. The time too – the hands on the clock in front of me moved as if they were in mud. The beeping noises of the machine, the robins outside, the noisy shoes that worked the floor tiles of the hospital, they all threw me into a state of fury and madness.

After two long enduring hours all that was left of me was a molten piece of manure of skin and bones. My mind crushed like a trampled leaf. Exactly then I received visitors.

"Heyo! Sorry about coming so late, but here we are!" Trina barged in. "How you doing *ol' sport?*" she threw herself on the chair beside me.

"Now that you're here, incredible," I somehow forced out a little smile.

"Not only have we brought you the fresh clothes that you so begged for, but also…"

"Cake!" Roland carried a round chocolate cake into the room. "We know you love chocolate. Plus, guess what, it's with marzipan!"

I really was grateful, but I couldn't show it.

Roland plopped the cake onto the nightstand beside me. "We spoke to the nurses; you're allowed to leave. So, eat up, and let's go!"

I shut my eyes, wishing I remained a molten piece of manure. "I don't want to leave. I can't."

"Yes, you dummy. Yes, you can, we've asked." Trina laughed. "Or do you have some weird fantasies we don't know of?"

I then realized I could move again, and with faint energy I sat up, still with a soaring headache I dangled my feet over the floor. Trina saw the splashed tears on the floor and quickly changed up.

"Kale. Why are you crying?" She held my hand and sat next to me on the bed. "We're here for you."

"Thank you for all this, but I can't –" my lips trembled.

"What is it?" Roland said.

"Hanna is gone."

"How gone?"

I passed them my phone with the messages I had received.

The air suddenly thickened, and I could feel Trina's breath cut, as she began to cry. Roland embraced her, keeping himself together as much as he could. The room was quiet for a long time until the nurse came to clean up the room. I got dressed and Roland took the cake and gave it to a random person. No words were being spoken, the look was all we needed.

We split paths to go home. It was starting to darken by that point. I entered my small apartment, closed the door and threw the keys somewhere. I sat down on the only couch I have and stared in front of me. The window was still fogged up. The droplets hung there for dear life. Slightly rotten wood frames held it all in place, strengthened by cold steel that took some punishment. It had three major scratches, all of which were to thank me for. It laughed at the curtains beside it, that I have never washed. They screamed at me for my negligence. I would rip them from their misery one day. The fabric, that once was deep blue was murdered by the sunlight. Its faded nature welcomed tiny fabric balls that peeled off and fell on the carpet to vacuum. They screamed at me too. Not only could I hear it, but I could also smell the unwelcoming scent of it. Like a two-star hotel in the mountains. Skiers bring in their stinking socks, the yellow wall lamps, a breeding ground for moths and all sorts of things, and the endless rustle of ski trousers and thick jackets. I never liked skiing, nor the culture. Everything seemed so sweaty and annoying. Just like my office chair, which was built before the invention of cassettes. Its harsh noises when turning could deafen a dog, so not only could I not sit properly, but I couldn't dare to move as well. I might have to throw it out the window.

When I came to my senses, I was panting hard. In front of me the living room took my wrath. The window was shattered, the curtains were torn and stained all over. The missing chair was found beside the street, still in one piece, but bent to a degree of no repair. Despite that, there were shoe prints all over the wall and shelves and cupboards were leaning against the walls.

There was a knock on the door. "Is everything fine in there, Mr Ingram?"

I didn't care to answer, but I kept seeing his shadow invade the slit beneath the door. So, I opened the door eventually.

"Yes, everything's fine." I said, focusing on his used home slippers. "Sorry for the noise, I will be quiet now."

"Noise? You broke a damn window! You better fix that. I will not live in a junkyard."

I just stared at his skinny calves.

"Listen to me. I don't know what went wrong, but you can't be behaving like this. I will let this slip because you look awful. I want the window fixed by next week, or I'll call someone, you hear me?"

Yes, I did indeed 'hear him', but whether I cared was another story. His slippers turned to the side towards the stairs.

"I will be checking in on you about that. You want to fix yourself up, you're bleeding onto your T-shirt."

"I'm sorry for your inconve-" I shut the door.

The window was indeed a problem, as the chilly air of the night would have free entry. But I figured it wouldn't faze me, as I already felt cold.

I sat down on the couch again and spent until morning the next day not sleeping for a single moment. The chaos was my waking companion.

I got up and opened the freezer to take out a frozen panini. I opened the packet and put the panini into the microwave, settings on full, for three minutes. It was still ice cold in the middle and tasted like nothing. Bland to oblivion. I left the dishes wherever they were when I finished eating. I covered the broken window with what was left of the curtains.

My mobile phone rang somewhere in the flat. The caller waited for a long time until they hung up. They tried three or four times, but I preferred laying on the ground with my back leaning against my couch.

When I was forced to stand up in order to go to the bathroom, my eye caught my work timetable I attached to the wall. I hoped I had something that would save me from myself, but my next shift was tomorrow morning.

In the bathroom I didn't even dare to look up to the mirror. I washed my hands, looking down at the partly rusted tap and my dirty T-shirt and pants. My fingernails were rough around the edges and dirty. My palm had calluses from which the skin was peeled and torn off. I turned the squeaking tap off and left the bathroom, that was still partly illuminated by second-hand sunlight.

There was an itch all of a sudden. It made me uneasy, and so I twitched and rummaged around to see what could get rid of it. I tried putting on the TV, but it didn't work. I tried reading, which failed almost immediately. Browsing the Internet didn't do it too, neither did Sudokus or any other puzzles for that matter.

In a fit of tired rage, I put my shoes on and threw myself out of my own flat. I saw the chair that still laid on the pavement. I took it and placed it beside the garbage bins. I did that in a rush. I thought of where to go, but just thinking of that made me clench my fists, so I just jogged straight and took any turns that were most convenient.

My breath echoed in my ears, it grew heavy very quickly. My feet were sore and my calves cried for mercy. But I felt the itch extinguish slowly. I passed the shops, the cemeteries, the schools. I ran through the park and ended up at a small place of greenery. It had trees scattered sparsely, with bushes and dead leaves filling the voids. I stopped not because of that, but I just couldn't go one step further. I dropped on the dead leaves and just buried my face into them, still breathing heavily.

The sunrays peeked between the leaves and branches of the trees above. My T-shirt, that had tucked itself out of my pants during the run, folded uncomfortably under me. I had no energy to move. I fell asleep.

Not sure how long it had been, but I woke unwillingly, as the sun, now a couple branches further, shone right into my face. When I moved, I felt my keys attempt to pierce my thighs. That drove me insane for a split moment.

I had no idea where I was. I roughly knew which way to go, but I didn't see anyone, not even a path or direction of any sort. Just way back through all the tree trunks I could see an opening field, presumably from the park. Naturally, I made my way there.

Through the park I eventually found a road I knew well. It was afternoon, and people stared at me. My clothes were begging for to be thrown in a fire, with all the scratches, tears, dirt, and stains. My face was beaten up obviously too, but I didn't care about any of it.

Commuters passed me in wide turns, some even crossing to the other side of the street in sight of me. I fidgeted my keys in the pocket all the way home.

Sluggishly, I took off my clothes as soon as I closed my apartment door behind me. I turned the shower on and stayed there for a long while. Looking down at my feet, I could see the dirt spiralling down the drain. It was when I washed my face, I could feel how sore my nose and left cheek were. They felt swollen and upon touch a swift pain emerged. I finished up and dried myself off, catching a glimpse of myself in the mirror. I could see who I really was. The black eye and puffed cheek. The stubble emerging around my split lip. I brushed my teeth for the first time since the event. I made sure to get all the corners thoroughly. I put some shorts on as soon as I finished and passed out in my bed.

It was 2am in the morning when my mind decided to begin the cycle anew. I made some breakfast and slowly but surely cleaned up bit by bit, until there was only the broken window left and the stubborn stains by whatever it was. I dealt with them too. By that point I was relieved, because I could start my commute to my work.

"Good morning," Anthony said, turning his squeaky desk chair to me.

I didn't say anything, not looking at him, trying to hide my face. I took off my jacket in one swing and just threw it toward my desk. It hit the cupboard behind my chair, as I left the office.

The dome was silent. Butterflies were hiding in the thick bushes. The gentle arrival of dawn. I could finally breathe. I could feel such weight bleed out of me with every gasp.

I leaned on the wall next to the door and delved deep into my thoughts. I could see my mum and dad. I could see Ada and Marcelina, all of whom I hadn't heard from for a long time now. I reminisced all the joined breakfasts we had, all the times we said "I love you", "Good night", "I'm sorry". Every time I went to school and saw the same teacher, the same friends. I could sense the rough wood from my school desk, from which so many hours were spent, but so little could be remembered.

I could see the saddened faces of disappointment looking at me. The obvious regret in putting faith in me. The anger of wasted time. And from the endless crowd one face emerged that struck an immediate sense of urgency. It was Ela, and with a cigarette in her mouth she uttered these words coldly:

"What are you going to do about it? Ears up!"

A rush of air woke me up from my daydream. The door next to me slammed closed.

I sat there silently, wondering what Anthony was doing. I couldn't hear him. When I peaked to my side there was a small paper bag. In it I found two chocolate doughnuts and a bottle of my favourite juice.

I bundled the paper bag in a tight ball when I finished picking up the chocolate crumbs. I opened the door and threw the ball into the trash bin across the room.

"First time I see that." Anthony said sitting up from his slouched reading position. "You don't have to be here today if you don't feel like it, *son*."

"Thanks Anthony." I sat on my chair not daring to look him in the eyes.

"Oh my! Your face!" Anthony stood up rapidly. "Let me see, we have a first aid kit."

I was too embarrassed to turn to him, so I kept looking down.

"Please, let me see." Anthony said, now standing right in front of me.

When I looked right at him, I could see him flinch with surprise, then squinting his eyes in sympathy and pain.

"I got punched," I said.

"Wow… It must've been a serious one. It looks like you got hit with a crowbar. I will put on some cream. I know there is some in the kit."

He got the cream and started applying it. "If you don't mind me asking – was there a reason for you to get hit? I know you had your ball. At my ball, years ago, there was a lot of drama – drunken drama."

"Yes, drunken drama," I said.

"Say no more." He finished and went to wash his hands in the small bathroom we have right in our office.

Quickly he stormed out drying his hands. "We got work to do, let's get cracking."

And without any desire whatsoever, I just followed Anthony through the shift. It felt like setting up the autopilot. I did what I always did, walk around looking at plants, being the best plant nurse possible. No words have been spoken in the dome, not even a glance shared.

Hyper-focused I ripped out dying plants, sprayed against diseases, even when there was just a speck of proof. Every thrust with my spade was stronger, crashing against hopeless roots, flinging out dirt everywhere. Hanna kept invading my mind and all the happenings started to flood me again. The damn ball, the stupid alcohol, everything! In that growing rage, a voice appeared in my mind, echoing in my skull: *"Why didn't you just stay? She asked you to stay. She needed yo-"*

At some point, deep into the sweaty work I was interrupted.

"Kale!" Anthony stood at my side.

I had just ripped out a plant like always.

"What Anthony!?" I shouted. "What is it?!"

"Did that plant really deserve to be replaced? Show me the reason." My buckets were overflowing with plants.

"Here." A little speck of brown on one leaf of a glorious flower.

"Oh, and that deserves the death sentence I understand?"

I just went on with ripping away the roots.

"Kale, your shift is over, and you haven't even started planting yet."

"Mhm," I continued.

"Stop Kale, this instance!" His voice rose. He took the buckets and left them by the biological waste bins.

I took off my gloves and threw them into the dirt, now following him into the office.

"What is it?"

"Sit down please." Anthony calmed his voice near to instantly. "I understand that you're not in the best headspace, but if it's affecting your work, it becomes a problem. Soon the first visitors will enter, and you know how much we care to show them beauty..." He stood over me. "... Not holes and earth-covered pathways. I have never seen you like this, so I know it's serious."

He took his chair and swung it in front of me and sat down. "Can I lend an ear perhaps?"

"I just need this. Really, I just want to work."

"There is no shame in sharing, *son*. We all have a button on us, which, if pressed, brings us to our knees…" I looked down to my hands.

A nice, new pair of gloves suddenly dropped on my knees.

"Kale, do what you must. I will go and oversee the opening of the zoo." He stood up and winked. "The plants and butterflies need you as much as you need them."

I looked at the clock and sprinted out to sort as much as I was able. My mind now like a spreadsheet filled with objectives, I hurried to fill the holes I made with new plants, dusted the paved walkway, and took all the tools into the garage.

The first wave of smiling visitors greeted me, while I pushed the dirty wheelbarrow around the long corners. I hid my face with my slanted hat. As soon as I was done with absolutely everything, I changed back into my normal clothes and headed out, without a sight of Anthony.

I got home to realise that I had left my phone in the flat since the ball. I was so into my thoughts that I didn't need the constant companionship of music. I found it under a pile of clothes that was thrown around multiple times. I picked it up to remember the completely cracked screen. So many notifications exploded right in my face when the screen lit up. Roland and Trina messaged me and called me multiple times.

Among others Ada wrote to me as well, which I responded to first. She usually wrote to me every couple weeks, to keep at least some contact. She asked me how I was doing which I responded with the usual positive. Knowing she would want me to elaborate, I briefly added the experience of the ball and how great it was. I felt bad not telling her everything, but I felt like I couldn't burden her with the worry of her older brother being in pieces. Thinking of her perspective, my guilt made me respond to Roland and Trina soon after. I arranged to meet up with Roland next week.

When I scrolled through all the trivial app notifications, at the very bottom appeared Hanna's voice message. The same haunting pictures flashed through my mind, but this time I promised myself to not push that aside. I sat down on my bed and listened to it. It was thirty-eight seconds long, and quite intoxicated she said:

"H-hey! Thank you for – for inviting me. I had loads of fun… It's a shame you didn't stay, but – what I mean to say – is that I really like you, and you are a very special person. It sounds a bit corny, but it's true. Warm hugs, and I hope to see you soon."

Between the last word and the end of the voice message I could hear a rattling of some kind. My throat choked up and my lips started to tremble. The phone screen wasn't dry for long. My walls echoed the message repeatedly, again and again:

"H-hey! Thank you for…"

When the sun started to descend, hiding behind the tree on the other side of the street, I figured I should eat something. I turned off the phone that surely grew tired of Hanna's voice. When I opened the fridge, I stared at 3 cloves of garlic and one shrivelled tomato in the back, on which green stuff began to grow. I opened the freezer and empty, ice-walled shelves greeted me there. I took my keys and headphones, threw something else on and went out. I didn't feel like walking, so I stopped at the bus stop a few steps from my front door.

I was still fumbling with my headphones in my pocket when I realised that I hadn't charged them. A flashing red light while trying to turn them on did prove it. Now I was standing at the stop in a group of people waiting for the goddamn bus. I didn't care about hiding my face anymore, they were strangers that I couldn't give any damn about. I overheard their pity problems and moaning. An elderly woman to my right sung the same old songs of taxes and government. I took a glance at her after a while and I thought of ploughing her head onto the curb, while imagining her partner's face of fear and surprise. I could feel my neck stiffen and I clenched my fist.

I switched my attention to the broken bricks I was standing on. My right foot pivoted side to side, as a piece of brick was all wobbly. Suddenly, I was aware of all annoyances on my body; the sleeve of my sweater under my jacket had slid up my arm, there was something in my boot that I failed to smash with my toes, possibly a rock. My sweater was choking me slightly, and my underpants rubbed on my inner thigh. First, the brick had to go. I bent down and pinched the wobbly piece and pulled it out. I threw it onto a small of patch of grass behind the bus stop.

I turned away from all the gazers and pulled my underpants down a notch by pinching my trousers. I left out a sigh of relief. I took off my jacket and slammed my right heel onto the same curb where the woman's face should've been. The pebble moved to the back of my boot, where I could fish it out.

"*Finally,* the bus arrives. With a 2 minute delay, the bus driver doesn't make a good impression," the woman continued to merit the face smash more and more.

She smacked at the driver while he pulled in. As soon as the doors opened, we all pushed in, knowing already that no one would want to step out. They rarely did at this bus stop.

Of course, all seats were taken, and I needed to stand next to the woman. I turned my back to her, holding the rail above me. The squeaky doors closed, and the bus accelerated. By this time, I knew the ride would be rocky, the driver didn't drive smooth at all. He didn't have a steady foot.

I wasn't the only one who recognised this, as I saw many annoyed faces in the bus. Some of them were lifeless, I guessed that life sucked them dry and were in a gruesome cycle. Just under a flickering light there was a couple sitting with their back to me. He put his head on her shoulder, while she looked out the window, scanning at the things that zoomed past. I wonder where they were coming from, or where they were going to. The movies? A party? Or maybe the park? I couldn't think for long, because a sudden stop challenged everyone to keep their balance. Even those who were sitting on these dusty, old chairs nearly smashed their heads on the guard rail. I leaned on the woman behind me that still kept talking smack about everything and everyone.

"Watch it!" She said to me, slamming her elbow on my back.

Who the hell did she think she was? I really wanted to say something, but somehow I kept it in me. I just turned to her slightly and gave her the meanest look I could muster. I wasn't sure whether it worked on her, but I thought it had some effect, because she didn't talk to me again. What a blessing she gave me there.

I stepped out the bus when I saw the large car park appear. My usual grocery shop was here too, but I had no fond memories whatsoever. It was my least favourite chore, and so I just grabbed what I wanted and went back.

Shuffling on the freshly mopped, still damp tiles, I squeezed through the slow elderly, the disappointed children putting toys back on the shelves, and a married couple unsure what they had on their forgotten shopping list. The freezers were on the other side of the damn building. I wasn't sure what to get in the end.

I took some frozen burgers, pizzas, and a bucket of ice cream. I got the bus again, but that time, luckily, everyone was quiet and depressed. My kind of company. Plus, there were seats available.

At home I put the burgers in the freezers and began baking the pizzas in the oven. Didn't have to be perfectly cooked through, it just had to be quick. I was already making good progress with the ice cream when I took the pizza out. The dough still looked a tad soft and pale, but that did the trick. I sat down on the couch, and with multiple movies this was how I spent my time.

Chapter Nine

I t was time for me to meet Roland. We met at the park and sat down between two food trucks, "in case we stay for long and get hungry," he reasoned.

"You look somewhat better." Roland inspected my face. "It was a real shock when I entered your room in the hospital. I didn't want to say anything, neither did Trina, but you looked beaten up bad."

I gave out a forced chuckle.

"Trina told me to tell you that you should perhaps think of covering your black eye with make-up. She said that the bruise will stay for a week or two, might as well learn how to cover it up."

"Thank you," I looked at the people ordering from the food trucks. The one to the left was a classic one, with hotdogs, hamburgers, fries and all sorts of those things. The one to the right had wraps, spicy things I had no clue existed, and exotic sides. The spices attacked my nose.

"What have you been up to?" I asked when the silence grew too long for my comfort.

"Well… nothing too interesting. Given that – you know, we both had to take some time away from everything else to digest it. A lot of sitting, a lot of thinking. I guess it is much harder for you though. I'm sorry to ask about it, but I have to – you know, being your pal - how have you been coping?"

I rarely saw that type of Roland. Sincere and patient. No flavour of jokes whatsoever. No hint of funny judgement.

"How should I feel man? I feel like shit."

"That's understandable."

"Why me? Like… what have I done to deserve this? I barely get a chance of being happy, and it gets taken away from me." Roland didn't answer, but he enveloped me with his left arm. "There are moments where I wished – and I feel so guilty about this – that I'd never stepped into the café for the first time. That I'd never met her."

"No, don't say that *man*. There have been many bad things, especially recently, but there has been a lot of good coming out of that as well."

I didn't know what he meant. There was a dark impenetrable mist in my mind. Sadness, anger, and all the flashbacks tormented my senses.

"You know…," he probably saw my confused expression. "It was exciting, wasn't it? I mean, it was something completely new to you. I know having new experiences is something you're not the most comfortable with… Also, you could learn how it is to be with someone. It isn't all that straight forward, but it must have been something worth learning."

"Yeah, I mean. Probably you're right." The dark fog still threw me off, but I began seeing flashes of incredible scenes; the park dance, the day with her at work, the café.

Roland kept talking about the good things. He even mentioned what his and Trina's perspectives were. "It was so fun and exciting for us as well!" He mentioned. "Awkward in some parts, but that was really wholesome to see."

"Thank you by the way." I fiddled with some grass I plucked from beside me.

"Thank you for what exactly?"

"For making me ask her to go to the ball."

"Oh." I could see him trying to figure out what he was supposed to say, balancing on a thin rope it seemed. "I'm glad to hear it. I kind of forced you... Oh, and that brings me to another thing: without all of this, you wouldn't have known what it was like to really like someone."

"I loved her," I winced.

Roland leaned forward, looking at the ground. "I figured."

"I loved her," I repeated. "Every time she came to me with her curious eyes, I didn't know what to do. I wanted to run, but also stay. I wanted to say nothing, and yet I wanted to tell her everything. From how I have been, to where I worked and what I liked. I actually felt useful for once. To be there for someone else, who wanted me to be there in the first place. I didn't know it at first, what I felt. But now with it gone, all I want is for it to come back."

Roland leaned back on the bench. He answered me with silence, so did I reply in the same way.

In that silence it became obvious how bustling the place had become. People eating food while standing, sitting on fences or benches. The food truck staff busy in their peak performance. We listened to them shouting out order numbers and asking for what the next customers wanted to order. The card reader was so loud, I unconsciously counted the beeps whenever someone paid. Like a table tennis game, the food trucks responded each other's beeps. In the end it was the hot dog stand that won, with 16 beeps compared to the other's 12.

As soon as the queue broke away and scattered all over the park, the backdoor of the food truck from both sides flung open. From the spicy truck a middle-aged woman came out, already with a pack of cigarettes in her hand. From the other one, a tall young guy, like me or Roland stepped out in the mist of his e-cigarette.

"Two gladiators in the ring." Roland said, seeing the same thing as me.

"They have similar weapons too."

Both of them heard us. The guy to the left laughed.

"You bet!" He said. "We do this nearly every week. We are enemies, and friends at the same time, aren't we Carol?"

The woman looked up and took a deep puff, then exhaling it through her nose. "Oh yes, my nemesis."

"Aren't you hungry?" the guy said, after again inhaling the e-cigarette, that just now we were able to smell the blueberry flavour from.

"Not really," I responded.

The woman threw down her cigarette, which was only half done, and went back to the truck. "I'll give you something to snack boys," we could hear her say through the thin metal walls of the little factory.

"Don't you think I know what you're doing?" The guy said, stomping in his truck as well. "I'll give you something too."

Roland whispered something to me, but I didn't quite catch it. I nodded at it, trying to bluff myself out of it. It seemed to work.

Shortly after, they both came out of their foodtrucks, the woman giving a basket of nachos with some spicy looking sauce next to it. She gave it to Roland. The tall guy had a big hotdog, which he gave to me. It was plastered with sauces, caramelized onions, and some pickles.

We both thanked them profusely. Even though it wasn't necessary at all, they insisted.

"Don't you worry guys, it's no big deal. It doesn't seem you had a good time," referring to my face I assumed. They both smiled and bumped fists making their way into their food trucks again, as people started queueing.

"Man, how nice of them!" Roland looked at me, and then the nachos. If he'd be a cartoon, his eyes would transform into pulsing hearts.

We finished the meals without saying anything in between, except for the occasional grunts, slurping, and munching. When we finished, we threw away the trash and gave each truck a tip and thanked them again. They didn't want to receive it, but this time we were the ones insisting. For the longest time since the ball, I forgot of what happened and we talked about everything else. Even the most absurd things. Roland and the fading taste of slightly burned onions in my mouth carried me along, until we stood in front of Roland's main door.

"Do you want to come in? I know it wasn't really the plan, but since you're here already, it wouldn't hurt. Trina is in too; you could say hi."

I thought about what else I had to do today. There were a couple things, but none of them really sprang to my highest priorities, so I agreed.

Roland opened the door, and we could hear Trina from a room. "Wondered if you'd come in Kale. Saw you through the blinds."

Roland took off his shoes in a flash and went in the room. I could hear them talk in a low voice, but couldn't make it out what they were saying. Not really a nosy guy, so I just focused on loosing my shoelaces and placing the shoes neatly next to all of the others. Trina came out of the door with three boardgames in her hands.

"Let's play some games, yeah? The living room is free."

As I walked along the hallway, Roland shut the door of the room and smiled.

"What do you want to play?" Trina laid out everything quickly on the table. But when she had placed everything, waiting for my response, I could see her hand shaking. Roland came over and took her hand, squeezing it tightly; his tip of his fingers turned white from the pressure.

"You forgot something Trina." I pointed to the boardgame I wanted to play.

"What?"

"What about a hug?" I tried a smile, not sure how it looked, as her jitteriness made me anxious too. I could feel the dim cloud in my mind coming back. My shoulders felt heavier.

"Oh! Of course! Roland, get something to drink, won't you?"

As Roland went to the kitchen, Trina came for a deep hug. "Thanks for coming," she said through my shoulder in which she was buried. "Let's have some fun for a change."

We then proceeded to play, round after round. The roll of the dice, the rivalry, the background music, all of that caught my dark cloud like a lasso and dragged it away. Trina's hands were not shaking anymore, and her cockiness and explosiveness kicked back into gear.

It was then that I noticed that I wasn't the only one who was hurting. All this time. I knew it wouldn't make things better, far from it, but somewhere in the back of my mind it was a thin blanket covering me. With that thin blanket in my mind, I went to sleep that night very deeply, after I won the board games.

Over the next days the heaviness returned, but it became a passenger I got used to, and so I could walk, talk… think more easily. I took the advice and bought some make up which I put on every morning. Luckily my face healed rapidly, so my horrible cover ups didn't need to be used for long.

Clothes were lying around everywhere. They needed a wash. Opening my tiny utility room, I checked how much detergent was left in the big bottle. It was empty. Then I also remembered that I had little toilet paper left as well, so grocery shopping was a must.

I didn't have long till the shops closed, so I had to get the bus. I tried to check the bus timetable on my phone, but the phone didn't turn on. I tried to reset it, clicking all sorts of buttons, but nothing. I took out the sim card and put the phone into my drawer. I remembered I had my older phone somewhere in the flat. It was slow, but it would work for the time being.

In my cupboard were a couple boxes, filled with winter jackets, scarves, books, and all kinds of junk. The first two I opened were full of clothes, but when I opened the third, unwinding cables popped out. That was a good sign. I put all the unnecessary stuff to the side, revealing the phone, which lay on top of my old console. I was surprised to see it and took it out too. I then decided that I could do the chores the next day.

Next to it was a white cloth for some reason. I grabbed it and it turned out to be the T-shirt with chocolate stains on it. I held it tightly, remembering Ela and all what had happened a long time ago now.

I dusted off the console and opened the disc reader to see if there was a CD in it. I was hoping so because I had no clue where the games were. Inside I saw 'Parla de Taux', the second part.

I plugged it to my TV and turned it on. The light flashed green, and the motors gave out a loud sigh of liveliness. The TV picked it up and showed signal. The sound, the controller, all gave me a rush of memories. In the menu I saw there were saved progresses. I clicked on one of them, and the loading screen, with its catchy music, appeared.

I found myself in the tundra and I sighed out loud. I remembered that I never passed this stage and gave up. I moved around for a while to see if I could still remember all the buttons and their functions, and of course I died in the game. In fact, I died over and over, trying to traverse the bushes quick enough to avoid the relentless wolves that watched my every step.

Time flew by, as I tried to pass this mission, but I couldn't make it to the other side. In rare occasions I passed the bushes, but either I failed by freezing in the river trying to cross it or was hunted down at the river bank.

Hours in, after one particular death I threw down the controller.

"No wonder I didn't come back to this damn game," I spoke out loud.

I held my head and massaged my face aggressively. When I looked at the screen again, I realised that the throwing of the controller pressed a button to try again, and the game was on, with Parla waiting at the hillside I now knew so well.

In a bloodthirsty rage, I actively tried to kill Parla, by running into every bush I could see. It worked, with me trying again and again, to kill him faster. One faithful try, I turned around and went the other way that you're supposed to go. The bushes became sparser and on a large rock I could see something gleaming.

The wolves' howl echoed in the valley, and I knew I didn't have long until I had to restart again. I used up all the stamina to get to the rock, to see a butterfly too big to exist in reality.

Looking at it, I knew the developers were inspired by a species called 'Oeneis uhleri' or 'Uhler's Arctic'. When I stepped closer, it flew off traversing the rocks, which I followed of course. It flew into a large crack in the ground. I clicked on it.

I arrived in a dark mine shaft, illuminated by magical butterflies glowing in various colours. The mine shaft was overgrown with lively, green bushes. I went deeper, passed the first wooden frames of the shaft, still following the butterfly.

The walls showed scraping, and polished chipping, probably by the pickaxes and other tools. The path split into three directions, and the butterfly disappeared into one of the bushes. All of them looked the same, and lead into darkness, without any bushes, just heavy, old wooden frames.

I picked the one to the left. In total darkness, I tried to use my torch which was in the inventory, but it didn't let me. 'Possible flammable fumes and material' was the reason the game gave. I decided to just go with it.

It was a long walk until I could sense something. I could hear a rush of water, presumably above me. Faint howling was to be heard too. I pressed on, leaving the noises behind, and entering a larger space, lightened by cracks to the surface where the sun peeked through.

A lonely chest was there, which upon opening, gave me golden coins and an item. I left the underground by climbing an old ladder and barely opening a hatch. I stood on the other side of the valley, staring down the wolves that couldn't cross the river. The mission was complete as Parla could reach the next town in one piece.

I stood up in triumph and disbelief that I never tried to go the other way this whole time. I saved the progress and shut it off. My dry eyes were closing, and my mouth wouldn't stop yawning.

It was a month or so later, when I found myself in a spot of happy anticipation. Together with mum we arranged Ada's visit to mine. There was a lot of planning that had to go into it, considering I had to negotiate with Anthony as well, so I could get some vacation days. The summer was particularly busy for the zoo, so it was stricter about getting time off.

In the end it was all successful. She would be arriving next week for five days. I couldn't wait to see her again! The wait was too long, and during a call with Ada, I could hear her excitement too.

In preparation for her I needed to do a lot of chores. Stock up the fridge, buy her favourite sweets, clean the flat, put up my air mattress. I made a whole list and punched it on the wall with glue tack; it was 12 bullet points long. I went right to work and spent the day vacuuming everywhere, even moving the furniture, which I did less than I care to admit. I also cleaned the bathroom. I gave myself generous breaks, as there was nothing else, I had to do.

The days went on by slowly, but the list got checked off one by one. When I was hanging up my clothes on the drying rack, Ada called me.

"Kale! I can't wait." She screamed out as soon as I hit the green button. "I am so excited. I already packed!"

"You packed all by yourself?"

"Yes, I tried, but mum told me she will have a look later. She doesn't trust me."

"No, she does!" I said, stretching a T-shirt and hanging it. "She does that because I was so horrible. I guess I made it worse for you."

I heard her giggle.

"I'm preparing everything at the moment, so when you come we'll be all set. Tomorrow I will go do the groceries. What do you want to eat, and what sweets should I buy? The sour ones you like so much?"

"Yes!" she exclaimed, changing quickly to whisper. *"Can we have pizza? And please get loads of ice cream too."*

Mum made me promise to feed Ada healthy food, but allowed the occasional junk. As Ada wanted a break from healthy food, I didn't see anything wrong in getting a couple of cheat days.

"Of course, whatever you like."

"Mum is coming!" She said.

"Is that Kale! Say hi from me." I could hear mum say in the background. *"Don't speak for too long, we need to leave soon."*

They were going shopping to the mall, to get some new trousers, as Ada was getting taller by the minute!

"I heard," I said. "You know what Ada, let's end the call here, so you can spend a bit more time with mum. If you can't wait those few days, then call me again. But soon we can talk all day!"

Ada was such a wholesome kid. She hung up on me, but I knew she wanted to continue talking. My focus switched back to the clothes. I loathed doing chores without distractions…

I left the house the day before Ada would arrive. I knew that it was the only chance to buy her some doughnuts, because the bakery would be closed the next day.

I walked to the bakery and bought eight doughnuts of different kinds, so she could choose which ones she wanted. I knew they would be a bit stale when she would eat them, but it would be better than no doughnuts.

On the way back I saw the same church where I met with Hanna so long ago. I held the wrappers tightly, hoping she would leave the church any moment, but I fooled myself.

My heart began to race, and my breath became difficult to control. I clinched my hands, slightly squeezing the doughnuts I just bought. My eyes were fixated at the church doors in a deep tunnel vision.

A snap of rage made me gain control of myself again, but instead of walking home I went to the nearest bar to settle my nerves.

"Nice to see you again, darling. How have you been?" the woman from the bar recognised me.

"You remember me?" I glanced at her before I sat down in front of her at the counter.

"Of course! Who wouldn't remember you? You are the guy who tried to get a juice in this bar. The first and probably the only one for many more years to come." She hastily flipped the menu in front of me. "We don't have any chicken I'm afraid, but we have the same soup you ate last time."

"No. I will get something of a strong sort first. To drink I mean."

She smiled. "First time trying alcohol?"

Her nosy style became a chore, but I quickly realised that that it was exactly what I signed up for the moment I decided to walk in. It wasn't unbearable, but I just wanted to be alone and drink something.

"No. I want… this" I pointed at a bottle which was untouched. I knew it was, because it was full, and the tape or foil that wasn't ripped off at the top.

"You sure? It's quite hefty. Not many people drink this one."

I just stared at her thinking of whether I should be blunter in order for her to actually do what I was saying.

"Do as you wish." She opened it with one twirl and poured some of it in a bell-shaped glass. I took it and drank everything in one go as soon as she placed it onto the menu in front of me.

"That'll be 5 pounds," and as she said that my mouth had just understood what I have gulped. My eyes squinted hard, my tongue squeezed against the roof of my mouth.

"Seems like you're not the man for rum."

I gave her double the money in cash and asked for another. I wouldn't let her tell me what she thought she knew. I drank the same crap again, with similar effects.

"I'll have the barbeque ribs and the beer called 'Rattlecave'. This time with card."

She continued talking to me in this mum-ish tone, until two other customers sat down next to me and demanded rudely to be served. From then on nobody talked to me at all, giving me the chance to be taken away by the satisfactory ribs that were too salty, and the beer that tasted like a rusty break calliper of a dragster. Some weird folk rock was playing through used speakers from which you could hear a constant buzz. I stared at the opposite counter edge while I ate and drank.

I finished pretty rapidly and ordered some more liquor. She didn't talk to me much anymore, as the bar filled up person by person.

It was the moment I stumbled towards my seat coming back from the bathroom that I convinced myself I had enough. I made sure I got all my things and headed towards the door. However, three tall men opened the door first and energetically made way straight to the bar. The first man pushed me away and I fell onto a chair.

I was laying on the floor gathering my thoughts, feeling my hip that I smashed against the corner of the table. My left elbow wasn't too well either. I looked up and saw one of the men waving a hand pistol around. There was a lot of shouting, but I had to focus to make out the actual words. People were running away, pushing chairs, stools, and tables away from their path towards the door. It was only me, them, and the bartender in there, so naturally I clawed myself back up and as the adrenaline pumped, I leaped out of the door. Just when I turned one of the guy's grabbed my arm and pulled me towards him.

"Where the hell do you think you're going?" He laughed. His hand gripped my shirt tightly, revealing tattoos on his knuckles that followed under his long sleeves.

My heart raced and I froze. He kept me in his grasp like a dirty rag. One of his friends opened the door behind us, and without missing a beat his knuckles flew right into my face. The corner between the stone pavement and the outside wall of the bar became my world. Old used chewing gum, cigarette butts, little pebbles and dirt shifting with all the vibrations, as the same knuckles made me gurgle my own blood, striking me over and over.

"Enough," said the third who had three rings on both of his hands. "Leave him, he's had enough." What was only a blurred figure in the back, was the one who had shown me mercy.

"I don't think so," the red fisted gasping bloke said. He kneeled right in front of me, and with a swift metallic ting, he stabbed me in the stomach. "Have a nice one fella," he whispered to me smiling. He stood back up and stomped the wrapper full of the doughnuts that I dropped beside me. The jam and custard filling spurted out onto the pavement. They left running and disappeared.

My stomach burned more and more with every breath. Not being able to lift my head, I let go off my wound and raised my hand in front of me. Blood dripped on my face, and it flowed through my shirt quickly.

Looking at the doughnuts, all I could think of was Ada. I didn't dare to think of anything else, and the thought of her disappointment and sadness overcame me.

The door swung open again. It was the waitress. She immediately came to me and put pressure on my wound. I couldn't hear a thing; it all became quiet. I read her face, wide eyes and a talking mouth. She pointed outwards and handed over a phone to someone. I could not turn away from the ground, and when I became weaker, my face rolled on the pavement, until my nose stopped my head rolling further. The taste of iron and grit greeted my lips and tip of my tongue. She rocked me back and forth, but my eyelashes closed my sight like a curtain in a theatre.

Everything went dark for a moment until a blinding light appeared. On my feet I felt light pressure and my head could move freely. I was standing in a white abyss completely alone. There was nothing, or no one around me. I noticed that I was wearing the same clothes, but they weren't red anymore, nor was there the knife wound. While I was walking in search for something, I felt some resistance in my right thigh. Out the trouser pocket I took out a large white feather and when I did, a swarm of butterflies welcomed me, sitting on my head, arms, and shoulders. They poked a hole in the whiteness, from where they came from. I step towards it peeking through.

I saw cliffs and calm waves hitting against them, pulverising it into droplets. Like a fog in strong winds, the whiteness faded, and the butterflies flew away behind me. I was standing in a field with flocks of sheep grazing right by me.

"Kasbiele," I heard behind me. As I turned, the butterflies turned into a swarm of angels. "Brother, thank you for taking good care of us. Now let us take care of you," one of them said and stepped up to me. Like all the angels, I couldn't fully comprehend its beauty, but this particular angel was different. It had two pairs of wings and was grey.

"How nice to see you, finally," it hugged me tightly. Its dark grey, curly hair buried my face. It smelled just like the air after a great thunderstorm. But when I got its hair out my eyes, I could see the group of angels again, with one of them seeming quite familiar.

"I don't know what is happening," I said.

"Sure you don't brother. Soon you will understand everything. Please know, you are safe."

Then it flew away with all the other angels, except for the one that I spotted earlier.

"What a nice feather you have there." It pointed at my hand, floating towards me.

"I don't know what this means," I looked at it with confusion.

To this, it didn't say anything, but turned its back to me. On its right wing was one feather missing. I wanted to give it back, but it said to me, "Keep it, as a gift, and as a reminder. Now come with me, there is more to show you."

It led me far into the fields where the grass grew wildly, but somehow without any weed. Every plant had its place and all of them seemed to thrive. There were Daisies and Tulips to the left, Peony and Dandelions to the right. As far as the eye could reach, the fields changed in colour together with all kinds of flowers one could think of and some that I had never seen before.

"It's like a garden," I said, in awe of every flower being healthy and perfect. "Like someone has been taken care of them for a long time."

"The gardener would be quite spectacular." The angel smiled at me. "Given there are so many in need of help to grow."

"Oh, look at those over there!" I pointed. "What a wonderful species. What are they?" They were black with light blue spots sprinkled at them. The stem was lime green, with quite a few rounded leaves sticking out of them.

"You have to ask the gardener," it laughed out loud. "We can have a look."

As we turned from the grass into the flower patches, the stems bent away from me, clearing the path ahead, so there would be no need of trampling them. They were alive, too alive.

"Don't worry, it's a special kind of fertilizer that is being used. Do you wish to take one with you?"

I wouldn't dare normally to pick one out. They were all too beautiful together.

"I need to speak with the gardener first. I don't want to mess up anything."

"I'm sure that's alright. One flower among so many will not be a problem, don't you think?"

It did make sense, but which one was I supposed choose? They all looked so beautiful and close to identical. I looked around in the patch of black flowers that I still didn't have a name for. I wanted the one to be special. The angel beside me waited patiently and watched me rather curiously.

"Sorry," I said. "I can't decide."

"It's alright."

"Which one would you take out?"

"One that speaks to me, I suppose," it said.

"Yes, but how do you know it does?"

"Why won't you just ask the flowers and not me?"

"What?"

It showed its sparkling white teeth in a big smile.

"Trust me," it said.

It felt too weird to talk to the flowers out loud, so I mumbled it. I reached out for one that looked interesting, but when I stretched out my hand towards it, its stem bent away from me. So did the flowers next to it. I took a step and the same thing happened as before, they all steered away. I took another step, and another, and another, until I saw one flower stand proudly. It looked just like all the other ones, but it had fewer spots. When I reached out to it, it bent into my open hand and plucked itself free from the soil.

"This is your flower," the angel held on to my shoulder. "I know, truly, the gardener planted it just for you."

I was hypnotised by the flower's complexity. Everything was so right. Nothing was there to be improved or cut off. There were no darker spots anywhere, nor any little insects.

"Thank you, gardener." I raised the flower slightly in gratefulness.

We returned to the grass where soon we reached a cliff's edge. The scenery took my breath away. It was a lake, surrounded by cliffs and mountains, that could be seen in the distance. The sandy shore glistened in the sunset.

"The painter is nearly as good as the gardener." The angel held on to my hand.

"Perhaps even better."

"Don't worry," it said. "We will overcome this little obstacle." It opened its arms towards me and I accepted its hug. "I'm so proud of you."

It flew me down the cliff onto the lake's shore, which wasn't of sand, but of golden coins.

"Thank you," I said.

"No, thank you," it said. "We have arrived. I cannot go with you, even though I really want to."

"What? Why?"

"This last part - you will need to go by yourself."

I looked around me. "Where should I go? What should I do now?"

"It's for you to figure out," he looked onto the water intently. "Farewell now, brother. It's good to see you." It then flew up high, beyond the cliffs edge, leaving me stranded.

I looked around again to see if anyone else was around, but to no avail. I sat down on the hard coins that turned out to be of golden colour. I took one in my hand. It looked faded and worn. Even though it seemed of high value, I threw it to the side. The flower that I had with me, I inspected again. The stem so ripe and hard, yet the leaves were so fragile and soft. It was like stroking a baby's cheek. The sun, that partly fell beyond the horizon, painted the sky in warm colours in contrast to the thick clouds. The sheep started to group together, as the moon behind me began to show its presence. I laid down, taking in the grandeur.

When it darkened considerably and the sun lay entirely out of sight, there was still a light. It was faint, but it was there. I too could hear a loud shivering of leaves rustling, but there were no plants or trees in sight. As soon as everything went to sleep around me, the dim light became stronger.

"Is that...?" I mumbled to myself. I saw a large tree in the middle of the lake, but not on an island, it stood on water. Its branches were moving up and down from the breeze. Pink leaves fell and floated to my direction. They fell onto the water, right in front of me. I picked them up, and as I did, my fingers weren't able to submerge under water. Thinking I was mad I tried with my whole palm, and it too rested on the water surface, no matter how hard I pushed.

Ultimately, I tried a step, and then another. I was standing on water, amidst pink leaves. The tree looked wondrous next to the light, so I gravitated towards it. Just when I reached it, I realised how massive the tree was. It stood taller than any tree I've seen, with branches spanning far outwards.

Its stem - surely unmovable, no matter what waves would decide to rage.

I went around it, looking up; only a few stars could peak through the dense branches and leaves. On the other side I saw the origin of the dim light. It was a streetlamp, also on water, flickering in the night. Its buzz reminded of insects. Further around the stem a bench revealed itself, with someone sitting on it.

"Nice to see you again, Kale," she smiled. "Is that flower for me?"

Afterword

Wouldn't it be great to work with butterflies? I certainly think so!

Hello there my dear reader. I see you have made it back from the grand lake. This section holds the truth of how this story has transformed itself from a vague idea to a book. If you seek more information on the plot itself, I am dearly sorry to disappoint you – you won't find it here.

As hinted before, the main theme of this book sprung to mind while I was on my daily walk to the university library. To get there I had to pass by a cemetary, which sparked many emotions and thoughts through the years, but none was stronger than this - The idea of how my guardian angel views the world I am so accustomed to, and how their perception differs from everything I know. A guardian angel who saved me time and time again. When I was back home, I looked for such a book, but to no avail. And just so I forgot all about it, until a tragically beautiful dream found me anew, many nights later. Perhaps it was my guardian angel, but from that point I knew that some things were indeed *meant* for me.

The writing process was squeezed between university work and other hobbies. I remember distinctly realising what a massive undertaking the book would be when I finished writing my first chapter. It wasn't the "leisure activity" I thought it would be. So, naturally, I took it more seriously.

Despite short parts being written at home overseas, the vast majority was written at the *Sir Duncan Rice Library* in Aberdeen. It was my second home in many regards. I had a clear vision of what the story looked like, I just had to describe it on paper. I took great inspiration from my family, more specifically my unique relationship with each member and our collective culture and behaviour. Even though this book doesn't describe real scenes, I allowed some truths to leak into this story. For instance, multiple characters are named after some of the members of my family, as this, for me, massive undertaking would be devoted to them. One in particular, Grandma Ela, was and still is such a big part of me that I realised I could only do her justice by putting her true self into the book. Grandma Ela became the only character based entirely on her real persona. Many phone calls were devoted with my mum and aunt to get to know my grandmother more, because she had died when I was eight. This book had become a family reunion.

Rather weirdly, I was never drawn to books before. Reading little in the past was a horrible habit of mine, which to this day haunts me somewhat. Due to this I knew I couldn't get inspiration from this media. So, I doubled down, and relied on something in me to drive me forwards. Similarly to my family, I let my own ideas take hold of the book, no matter how ridiculous some things may have seemed. I let go, and steered totally by what my angel told me to 'see', I wrote scene after scene. And after an isolating and devouring surge of a little infectious idea in my head, the book was written.

I would like to thank my friends Max, Victor, Hannah, and Ella for their help in the editing phase, and for giving me the self-confidence and strength to finish this piece.

Printed in Great Britain
by Amazon

34277897R00133